RUTHLESS HUSBAND, CONVENIENT WIFE

MADELEINE KER

~ THE MARRIAGE BARGAIN ~

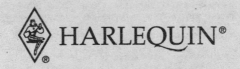

HARLEQUIN®

TORONTO • NEW YORK • LONDON
AMSTERDAM • PARIS • SYDNEY • HAMBURG
STOCKHOLM • ATHENS • TOKYO • MILAN • MADRID
PRAGUE • WARSAW • BUDAPEST • AUCKLAND

Recycling programs for this product may not exist in your area.

ISBN-13: 978-0-373-52724-3

RUTHLESS HUSBAND, CONVENIENT WIFE

First North American Publication 2009.

Previously published in the U.K. under the title THE ALPHA MALE.

Copyright © 2003 by Madeleine Ker.

www.eHarlequin.com

Printed in U.S.A.

RUTHLESS HUSBAND, CONVENIENT WIFE

CHAPTER ONE

IT STARTED being a bad morning when Hippy Dave backed his van into the workshop door at five o'clock in the morning.

Hippy Dave was one of Penny's less orthodox suppliers. He and his wife, Chandra Dawn, roamed the country, haunting village fairs. They also collected natural things that Penny could use for her arrangements, like interesting pieces of driftwood, bark, dried moss, dead bulrushes and the like.

They often came up with unusual material that Penny couldn't easily find elsewhere, so she welcomed their irregular visits. But she also suspected that Dave and the ethereal Chandra Dawn had other uses for the natural things they harvested; so when she heard the crunch of her workshop door being splintered by Dave's fender, she went out in a thoroughly bad temper.

'Dave! Have you been eating those magic mushrooms again?'

His tousled head emerged from the window of the rainbow-coloured van. 'Sorry, Penny,' he said shamefacedly. 'Wasn't concentrating.'

'Oh, Dave,' she said as she examined the damage. 'This is all I need!'

Dave hopped out of the van, wearing overalls and a pair of yellow boots. 'Just didn't notice the door was open, Pen.'

The workshop of Penny's florist shop opened into a mews, which was useful for deliveries, and where she parked her own smart little red van with its proud logo, PENELOPE WATKINS, FLOWERS & DéCOR. It had been while manoeuvring round her van, to get his own vehicle as close to the workshop entrance as possible, that Hippy Dave had caught the opened door. It now hung mournfully off its hinges.

'I'll fix the door, I promise,' Dave said, squatting to take a closer look at the damage.

'No, thank you,' Penny said firmly. She'd had previous experience of Dave's odd-job capabilities and knew she'd be better off getting a carpenter. And it would be useless asking Hippy Dave to foot the bill; he and Chandra Dawn were perennially broke.

As though reading her thoughts, Dave spread his grimy hands. 'Tell you what. You can have all the stuff in the van for free. Make it up to you, at least in part. OK?'

'You'd better get out of here before Ariadne arrives,' Penny said. 'She'll skin you alive.'

Dave's watery blue eyes widened as he contemplated the wisdom of this advice. Penny's associate Ariadne Baker, half-Greek and with a Homeric temper to match, was not one of his biggest fans. She had expressed her opinion of his shortcomings loudly and pointedly on previous occasions.

'Yeah, you're right. Look, let's get the gear out of the van. I brought you something real special this time. It's yours for nuffink.'

'Oh, don't bother. Just clear off.'

'Take it off my hands. Nobody else will buy this old rubbish,' Dave whined. 'I mean, this lovely natural object, sculpted by nature's own hand. Have a look, Pen!'

'Let's see what you've got, then,' Penny sighed, too depressed to want to look at the ruined door any longer.

Hippy Dave threw open the back door of his van to reveal what looked like an entire tree crammed in among boxes and crates.

'What am I supposed to do with that?' Penny asked blankly.

'It's lovely,' Dave said, hauling the thing out of the van. 'You'll see. There! What do you think of that?'

'I'm a florist, not a tree surgeon,' Penny said, looking at the enormous branch Dave had produced. 'This is no good to me!'

'Look at the shapes in there,' Dave said, half closing his eyes and waving his hands vaguely, the better to visualise nature's handiwork. 'That silvery bark is beautiful, and look at those strands of moss. That's magic, that is!'

'Dave, please take it away,' Penny said. 'I can't use it.'

'It's unique!'

'It's useless. I don't want it.'

Dave opened his mouth to argue, but just then a new voice joined the conversation.

'What's going on here?'

It was Ariadne Baker, who had just arrived, wrapped up against the frosty morning in a military overcoat, a cigarette in one hand, the other clutching a plastic cup of coffee she'd bought from a roadside stall on her way into town.

Twice-married and twice-divorced, Ariadne was a dramatically pretty woman around thirty, some seven years older than Penny, with jet-black hair and bright green eyes.

Those eyes hardened now as they took in the scene. 'What's that piece of dead tree for? And what happened to our door? Dave?'

Hippy Dave was not known for decisive movements, but a lifetime of evading the long arm of the law had given him a heightened instinct for self-preservation. He dropped the branch and hopped nimbly into his van.

'Be seeing you, Pen,' he called out of the window as the worn-out engine rattled into life.

And then the rainbow van was bounding down the mews, its still open back door waving a disreputable farewell to the two women.

'He's smashed our door!' Ariadne gasped.

'Yes,' Penny said.

'And he's left that rotten old tree for us to clear up!'

'Also true.'

'I'll have his guts for garters!'

'You'll have to catch him first,' Penny pointed out. 'He'll be halfway to London by now. Help me get the branch inside.'

'We don't want that horrible old thing in our nice clean workshop!' Ariadne exclaimed.

'No,' Penny said patiently, 'but we need to be able to get our vans up to the door. And we can't leave it lying in the mews or everybody will complain, and the council will fine us. So give me a hand.'

Ariadne's father was a retired colonel—he had met and married her Cypriot mother in Nicosia—and Ariadne expressed her opinion of Hippy Dave in choice, parade-ground language as they hauled the branch into the workshop.

It was, as Ariadne had pointed out, always kept spotlessly clean. There were three work benches, one for Penny, one for Ariadne, and one for Tara, the woman who helped out three days a week. There was a place for everything, and everything was in its place. Dried materials were stored in sheaves on wooden racks, there were large plastic bins for waste, and in the corner stood their most expensive piece of equipment, a climate-controlled cupboard for delicate fresh plants like orchids.

There was a huge sink crowded with zinc buckets for cut flowers, and a 'control corner' with their work book and a chalk board where they kept track of orders. Beside it stood a shelf for the kettle and mugs, which provided the constant flow of life-giving beverages—coffee for Ariadne and tea for Penny—which kept them going from before dawn till late afternoon.

The shop part of their business was partitioned off, and faced the High Street. It looked bare right now because they had yet to go to the market to buy flowers for the day.

'Damn Hippy Dave,' Ariadne panted, as they lugged the dead branch into a corner. 'He's a useless, addle-headed idiot!'

'We'd better get moving,' Penny said, checking her watch, 'we're late for the market. We can't lock the back door now that Dave has broken it. Why don't you go on your own, Ariadne? I'll stay here and try to get hold of Miles. Maybe I'll make some pot-pourri arrangements.'

'All right,' Ariadne said, dusting bits of moss and bark off her greatcoat. 'Arrange for a hit man to take Dave out, too, would you?'

'I'll dial M for Murder,' Penny promised. 'Here's the list, don't forget it.'

When Ariadne had raced off to the market, Penny perched by the phone and called Miles Clampett. He was sure to charge an exorbitant fee. He always did. They had met when she had done the flowers for his brother's wedding two months earlier. They had gone out for a few weeks after the wedding, but it had ended quickly, after his sense of humour wore thin on her. They were still on good terms. He was expensive. But he was the only handyman she knew who would come out right away, with no hesitation.

Though it was still well before six, she had no compunction about calling—this was an emergency.

A sleepy murmur answered her call.

'Miles, it's Penny Watkins. Sorry to do this to you, but Hippy Dave knocked my door off its hinges a few minutes ago, and I need a carpenter really, really, really badly.'

'Anything for you,' he yawned.

'You are awake, aren't you?'

'Yes,' he said.

'And you promise you'll come this morning? As in—now? We're in and out all day, and unless I can lock the place up—'

'All right, all right,' he groaned. 'I'll beam down from my spaceship. Give me half an hour.'

'Bless you,' she said, hanging up.

She made herself a cup of tea and set to work making room perfumers. It was undemanding work—arranging dried flowers in pots and sprinkling them with aromatherapy essences—but the arrangements were popular and sold steadily. She had an excellent eye for shape and colour, and she always had an assortment of pretty porcelain containers on hand. She put some of those to good use now.

By seven-thirty, her sensitive nose had had about as much as it could take of 'Floral Bouquet' and patchouli oil. She loved flowers and everything about them—their smells, their colours, their textures; but synthetic versions of any of those usually wearied her sensitive faculties, and that was particularly so with smells.

She went into the shop, pulling off her cap and untying her hair. It fell in rich auburn waves around her shoulders. Penny was slender and ivory-skinned, with dark blue, almost violet eyes and a full, slightly melancholy mouth. She was twenty-three, but it sometimes seemed as though she were still trembling on the brink of full womanhood, like a flower that had half opened, and was waiting for the clouds to part so that the sun could bring her to full glory.

There had certainly been clouds in her life so far. Not everything had gone right for her. But she had struggled to overcome adversity, and had usually succeeded, though the price she had paid was perhaps visible in that poignant mouth.

The blinds were still drawn, but through them she could see activity in the High Street. The town was waking up. Buses were running. It was turning out bright, though the rime of frost on everything had yet to melt.

She turned on the computer, and, while it booted up, considered this Wednesday in late autumn. It was going to be a busy day, and it would not help to have Miles underfoot, hammering and sawing away at the broken door, demanding tea every ten minutes.

There were several bouquets to make and deliver all over town. There was a funeral at one of the cemeteries, and several mourners had ordered wreaths and floral tributes. Though she and Ariadne had already assembled most of these, the finishing touches had to be made, and they would need to be taken to the chapel of rest well on time.

Then there was the mayoral dinner tonight. Penny was doing it for the first time, and she was anxious that nothing should go wrong. There was a lot of work involved, very little of which could be prepared in advance. For a start, there were sixty-five vases of fresh flowers to arrange, then the four tables themselves to set out and lay, plus the several larger flower arrangements that would greet the guests in the lobby and flank the high table.

She had long since agreed all the details with Her Worship's office, and she would need to be at the town hall by four at the latest, to start work.

She made herself her second cup of tea of the morning, and waited impatiently for Ariadne to arrive back from the flower market. There had been a lot of things to buy. Perhaps she should have gone with Ariadne. And where was Miles?

She heard the purr of a car in the High Street and looked up over her teacup. A steel-grey sports car, sleek and obviously very expensive, had pulled up outside the shop. Penny frowned, wondering who this could be, at this early hour.

The tall figure of a man got out of the car. She could not see him clearly through the blinds, but there was no question that he was looking into the shop windows as though to see if anyone was inside. She sat still, wondering why there was something so familiar about that tall, dark silhouette.

Then he knocked on the door. A hard, peremptory knock that made her heart sink. Getting a struggling business onto its feet had brought her into contact with all kinds of knocks on the door. Knocks like this one invariably brought trouble. She searched swiftly through her mind. Who did she owe money to? Had she left any taxes unpaid? Bills unsettled? She could think of nothing. Though she was still struggling, she had hoped she had left those precarious days behind her at last.

Her heart filled with unease, she went to the door and unbolted it. Cold morning air blew in her face as she swung it open.

'I'm sorry, we're not open yet,' she began to say. But the words froze in her throat.

She was looking into the unsmiling face of the handsomest man she had ever seen.

And also the last man in all the world she wanted to see.

'My God, I've found you at last,' he whispered, holding her gaze with those grey eyes that could be as cold as the Arctic sea, or blaze like the sun off ice.

Involuntarily, she took a step back. He came into the shop and closed the door behind them. He was much taller than Penny, and he towered over her.

'Ryan, you have no right to be here,' she said in a tight voice. But her heart was racing as though it would burst out of her chest, and she felt her stomach churning. Such familiar feelings, when faced with Ryan Wolfe; they accompanied him the way wild winds and lightning accompanied winter storms.

'Did you think I wouldn't find you?' he demanded, his gaze still locked on hers, as though he were drinking her in through his eyes.

Penny clenched her jaw. 'I didn't want you to follow me, Ryan. Why did you bother? What was the point?'

'The point is that I can't live without you,' he replied.

Her heart seemed to stop for a moment at the harshly spoken words, but she forced herself to answer him. 'Well, I can live without you,' she said with a sketch of a smile. 'I've been doing so for eleven months, two weeks and five days. Very happily, I might add.'

At last he tore his gaze away from her and glanced around the shop. His passionate, beautiful mouth curled. 'You're happy with this? When you know what I could give you!'

Anger brought a flush to her delicately sculpted cheekbones. 'Don't condescend to me, Ryan. Nothing is ever as good as what you can offer, is it? You hold everyone and everything in contempt.'

He shook his head slightly. 'That's not true. But I do know that I would give you the sun and the moon if you asked for them.'

She turned away. 'You're so sure of yourself. Haven't all these months taught you anything?'

'Time just deepens my feelings,' he said, his voice husky. His eyes were devouring her again, hungry, more than hungry, ravenous. Her skin flared in gooseflesh as she recalled how very physical his hunger could be, how he could devour her body and soul in that fiery passion of his. 'How could you do this to us, Penny? How do you manage to hide yourself from the truth?'

She turned back to him abruptly. 'You shouldn't have come here. Do you want to break both our hearts all over again?'

'I want to make us whole.' He took her arm in his hand, and as though his touch had burned her, Penny jerked away from him.

'Don't touch me!'

Ryan's frown had relaxed for a moment, but at her rejection his face tightened again. 'Do you know what you've put me through? It's taken me almost a year to find you! You've hidden here under a false name, a false identity—'

'Not exactly,' she cut in. 'Watkins is Aubrey's name. My stepfather. I'm entitled to use it.'

'You used it to hide yourself from me.'

'You should have taken the hint,' she retorted.

'Penny, you can't bury yourself here. You can't bury all the passion we feel for each other.'

'Passion dies, Ryan. I didn't have to bury it. It grew cold as soon as I managed to get away from you.' He began to speak but she stopped him by raising a slender hand. 'I thought you had understood, a year ago. It's over, forever. Your following me here was a bad mistake. Please go, now. And don't come back.'

If she'd expected her little speech to make any impact on Ryan, she was disappointed. Those grey eyes, framed by such thick black lashes that they gave the appearance of smouldering like embers, considered her with all their force, all their damnable intelligence. 'You don't love me any longer?' he asked quietly.

'I don't think I ever did,' she replied.

His hair was longer than it had been in London. Then, it had been cropped short and kept neat, as befitted a young, dynamic, self-made millionaire on his way up the dizzy ladder. Now it had grown. Thick black locks half covered his ears and curled round his powerful neck; dishevelled by the wind, his hair looked almost wild, like the pelt of some glossy animal. He had either made it to the top of the ladder, and no longer cared what he looked like—or this was a different, even more dangerous Ryan Wolfe from the one she had known.

The tall and rangy body, too, looked leaner, though it was hard to tell, as he wore a sheepskin jacket against the bitter cold. The fleecy lining framed his sculpted jaw and muscular throat.

Who knew, with Ryan? Perhaps he had lost a fortune in some disastrous gamble? He was studying her now with cryptic eyes, his thumb rasping across the unshaven stubble that dotted his lean jaw, a gesture she remembered of old.

'Penny, please grant me one thing,' he said, evidently struggling to keep his temper. 'I want to see our child.'

She felt an icy hand close around her heart. 'Our child? What are you talking about?'

'The child you bore,' he said sharply. 'The baby we made together. Where is he? Or is it a she?'

Her knees were so weak that she almost had to sit down. 'Don't pretend you don't know what happened, Ryan! That is cruel, even by your standards!'

His face became like stone. 'What happened? Tell me.'

She looked into his eyes. Could it really be that he didn't know? It was unlike him to play such cruel tricks, though he was capable of being very devious.

'There is no child, Ryan,' she said in a quiet voice. 'I miscarried.'

For a moment it seemed he did not understand. 'What?'

'I had a miscarriage at three months. I lost the baby.'

His complexion was usually tanned, with ruddy touches on the harsh cheekbones and in his full mouth. But now she saw the blood drain from his face, leaving him white. 'I don't believe you.'

She turned away wearily. 'I got sick. Encephalitis. I was in hospital for two weeks. One of the side-effects was the miscarriage. It happened while I was in a coma, so I knew nothing about it until days afterwards.'

His fingers bit into her shoulders, pulling her round to face his blazing eyes. 'Is this true?'

'I would not lie about this,' she said bitterly. 'Didn't you get my letter?'

'What letter?'

'I wrote you a letter. When I was discharged from hospital.' She saw by his face that he didn't know what she was talking about. He had never received her letter. 'I don't know why you didn't get it. I just assumed you had received it and didn't want to reply. I'm sorry you had to hear it like this.'

He covered his face with his hands. There was no doubting his emotion.

For a moment, pity for him almost melted her own heart. She felt her eyes mist over, and the familiar hot lump of grief filled her throat. She lifted one hand to reach out to him. Her shaking fingers hesitated in the air, not quite having the courage to make that journey across so much space.

At last, his hands dropped away from his face. 'Tell me the truth,' he said. 'Did you end the pregnancy?'

She was so shocked that she felt herself go limp for a moment. 'No, Ryan!'

'Did you get rid of our baby because you had no further use for me?' Pain and anger had brought his dark brows down, and his mouth was harsh.

'No!'

He grasped her arms so tightly that she knew there would be marks on her delicate skin. But far more painful was the expression in his eyes, which tore her very soul in half. 'Promise me!'

She opened her mouth to speak, not knowing what words she could use that would persuade him she had not done the terrible thing he accused her of.

But just then, the shop seemed to fill up with people.

Ariadne came in from the workshop, calling out, 'Pen, they didn't have near enough yellow gladioli, so I got cream, is that OK?'

And the shop door opened to admit Miles Clampett, carrying his carpenter's tool kit in one hand and two cartons in the other.

'I brought in your milk,' he said, his alert eyes flickering from Ryan to Penny and back again. 'Hello, earthlings! Hope I'm not interrupting anything?'

CHAPTER TWO

RYAN'S grip on her arms relaxed, and Penny stepped back.

'Cream gladioli are fine, Ariadne,' she said in a flat voice. 'Thanks for coming, Miles. The damage is out at the back. Ariadne will show you.'

Taking the hint, Ariadne led Miles through to the workshop. Both of them were clearly bursting with curiosity about their strange visitor and the palpable air of tension in the shop. Ariadne, who could be guaranteed never to let an eligible male pass unnoticed, gave Ryan an alluring smile as she passed by.

Ryan gave her a curt nod by way of reply, and as soon as they were alone, he turned on Penny with burning eyes. 'Penny, please swear that you are telling me the truth!'

'I refuse to swear anything,' she said, her lips numb. 'Why shouldn't you believe me?'

'You threatened you would end the pregnancy!'

'Yes, I know I said I would, but—'

'I didn't for a moment think you meant it.'

'I didn't mean it,' she said passionately. 'It was one of those crazy things people say when they're desperate.'

'You threatened to abort the pregnancy if I followed you,' Ryan reminded her brutally. 'Did I ever do anything to make you that desperate?'

'I'll say it once more,' Penny said with a sensation like an iron band around her heart. 'I contracted encephalitis. I almost died in that hospital. And when I was finally myself again, I had to deal with the loss of my baby. I would have done anything to avoid that. But there was nothing I could do!'

'Everything OK, love?' Ariadne asked, returning from the workshop, where Miles had started hammering industriously.

'Everything's fine,' Penny said in a dull voice.

Ariadne was staring at Ryan Wolfe with unabashed interest. In the few moments she had been in the back, Penny noticed ironically, she had found time to apply lipstick, brush her hair, lose the army greatcoat and unfasten the top button of her blouse to reveal the luscious curves of her breasts. In the absence of any inclination on Penny's part to offer introductions, she waltzed in where angels would have feared to tread.

'And this good-looking gentleman is…?'

Penny had no idea how best to answer that innocent question. My ex-lover. My nemesis. The phrases flitted through her head, but it was Ryan who answered.

'I'm a prospective client,' he said levelly.

'Oh, goody,' Ariadne purred. 'Do you live locally?'

'Yes.' He glanced at Ariadne. A peony to Penny's rosebud, Ariadne had curves that Penny would never match, and a co-quettish manner to go with them. 'I'm staying in Northcote Hall, on the Dover Road.'

'Northcote?' Ariadne repeated with interest. 'Oh, we know it well, don't we, Penny? Such a beautiful old place. Do you know the family?'

'I'm renting the house for the moment,' he replied. 'I may buy it if it turns out to suit my purpose.' He made it sound as though buying that beautiful country house was a mere baga-telle to him, and Ariadne positively glowed.

'That's wonderful news,' she gushed. She was reacting to

Ryan the way all women invariably did on first meeting him, Penny saw—greedy fish dying to bite that delicious bait, never seeing the steel hook that lay within.

Ryan shrugged slightly. 'The important thing is that I plan to do a lot of entertaining there. I'm not married, and I need someone to take care of my table arrangements, flowers, décor, that sort of thing.'

'Our speciality,' Ariadne beamed. 'Isn't it, Penny? We're the best there is.'

Whether Ryan had arrived with this story already concocted, or whether he was making it up as he went along, Penny couldn't tell. 'We're already far too busy,' she said in a clipped voice. 'I'm sorry, but we really can't take on any new clients at the moment.'

Ariadne didn't miss a beat. 'Please forgive my associate,' she said, patting Penny's shoulder, 'she suffers from a rare speech impediment that makes her say no, no, no when she means yes, yes, yes. How often were you planning on entertaining…? I'm sorry, I didn't get your name.'

'Ryan Wolfe,' he replied. 'And I generally need to throw at least one dinner party each week, generally on weekends. Around twelve people, sometimes more.'

'Perfect,' Ariadne said. 'We're all dying of boredom here. I hope you're going to bring all sorts of wonderfully interesting people to our little backwater! By the way, I'm Ariadne Baker. You obviously already know Penny Watkins. We're the best you could get, Mr Wolfe. Penny's doing the Lord Mayor's banquet tonight, as a matter of fact—the flowers, the place settings, everything. If you can take a peek into the Hall tonight around seven, you'll see what she's capable of.'

'I might just do that,' Ryan said meaningfully.

'I know she's just a baby,' Ariadne gushed. 'A mere twenty-three. But so much talent, and with me to guide her—'

'I understand,' Ryan said drily.

'When do you want to have your first dinner party, Mr Wolfe?'

'Well, I'm still refurbishing the house. It needs some tender, loving care. If I can get it looking halfway decent, I might ask one or two people to dinner on Saturday.'

'We do weddings on Saturdays,' Penny said shortly. 'We always have our hands full. Sorry.'

Ariadne squirmed. 'But we can make space! If you give us the job, your party will be beautiful, believe me. All your parties will be beautiful.'

'Sorry to interrupt again.' It was Miles, his arms sprinkled with wood shavings. He leaned in the doorway, giving them all the benefit of the knowing smirk Penny had once thought so amusing. 'Only, Hippy Dave has smashed your door good and proper. I'm going to need some planks.' He rubbed thumb and forefinger together meaningfully. 'The lumber yard won't give me credit for my handsome face.'

Penny felt like an automaton as she broke away from the conversation, which had taken a nightmarish turn. 'How much do you need?' she asked, opening her purse.

'How much have you got?' Miles grinned. Before she realised what he was doing, he came over to her and threw an arm familiarly around her waist. Pulling her intimately close, so he could look in her purse, he dipped a sawdust-coated hand deftly inside, and came out with three or four notes. 'This'll do,' he said.

While they'd still been going out, a few weeks back, that might just have passed as acceptable, but right now he knew he was about ten miles out of line.

And then he kissed her soundly on the cheek. 'Thanks, darling,' he said wickedly. 'For an earth woman, you are surprisingly un-hideous.'

He walked out, looking very pleased with his sense of humour. Of all the times for him to decide to play the fool! She caught Ryan's smouldering gaze on her, and felt his contempt. Unable to explain anything, she gave him a defiant look.

'I'm sorry to disappoint you,' she said coolly. 'Whatever Ariadne may think, we're very busy, and we won't be taking on any new clients.'

'Penny!' Ariadne said urgently. 'Of course we can take Mr Wolfe on!'

Ryan held Penny's eyes for a moment longer, then checked his watch, a wafer-thin sliver of gold she had not seen before. 'I have to be in London in two hours. But I'll be back. I will attempt to persuade you otherwise. I can be a very generous employer.'

'We're interested,' Ariadne said, obviously getting desperate as Ryan moved towards the door, 'we're very interested, Mr Wolfe! Won't you take one of our business cards?'

The grey eyes examined her. 'Please call me Ryan,' he said coolly. 'And I won't forget to come back. I'm sorry to leave so abruptly. My timing is a little off key lately. I hope you'll get used to it.'

'Oh,' Ariadne said, 'we can work around your schedule, I'm sure!'

Ryan nodded his thanks, then stared into Penny's eyes. His gaze was intense. 'I'll get back in touch. And when I do, I will want an explanation, Penny.'

His broad shoulders, snugly clad in sheepskin, swung through the door. It slammed shut.

Ariadne hurried to the blind to peer out. 'Look at that car! My God! Sex on wheels!'

'It's just a car, Ariadne,' Penny replied wearily.

'I'm not talking about the car, baby.' She watched as the sports car accelerated away, then turned to Penny with bright eyes. 'I never met anyone who was truly magnetic before. But that man is! If I was a bunch of iron filings I'd be coating him in a fine layer!'

'You practically were,' Penny retorted.

'It's going to be such fun working for him! Why are you so anti?'

Ariadne tilted her head on one side. 'You know him, don't you?' she said, her eyes narrowing to green slits. 'He didn't just walk off the street at eight o'clock in the morning. Who is he?'

'He's nobody.' Tension was slowly ebbing out of her. The shock of being with Ryan after nearly twelve months of separation—and all that had happened in that time—had left her feeling weak. She sat behind the desk and rested her forehead in her hand, feeling nauseous.

'Oh, yes, he's nobody, all right,' Ariadne said scornfully. 'The most wonderful hunk to ever set foot in this staid old town, and he's nobody? Who are you trying to kid?'

Penny looked up at Ariadne. Though Ariadne was practically a partner in the business, and a good friend, she knew nothing about her time in London or any of its consequences. She didn't know a thing about Ryan, about their break-up, about the encephalitis or the miscarriage.

And if she knew what Ryan's world was like, and the nature of the 'wonderfully interesting people' he was likely to bring to this staid old town, she would be even more stupidly infatuated with him.

'I knew him some time ago,' she said tersely. 'It ended badly. That's all.'

'I knew it!' Ariadne exulted. 'And now he's come back to find you?'

'I think it's just a horrible coincidence,' she lied.

Ariadne gave Penny a shrewd look. 'He's rich, right?'

'When I knew him, he was very rich,' Penny confirmed.

'So when he throws a dinner party, it's really a big occasion?' Penny made a face. 'Yes.'

'And he's going to do this every week? Honey, whatever happened between you and him, we can't afford to turn down that kind of money! We've got bills to pay, remember? Light, rent, flowers, the vehicles?'

'I remember,' Penny said, pressing her fingers into her eyes.

'So when he comes back to you—you are going to say a big yes, aren't you?'

Penny got up and walked out of the back. 'We've got work to do. Let's see these cream gladioli you've bought.'

'You will, won't you?' Ariadne pressed, catching up with Penny. 'You will say yes to the money?'

'Money is nice, isn't it?' Penny said, swinging the back door of the van open to reveal a colourful mountain of fresh flowers. 'But it depends what you have to do for it in return. Sometimes the price is just too high. Come on, we're late already, and we've got a lot of work to do.'

Ryan's arrival that morning had released a flood of memories and emotions that she'd been valiantly holding back behind some mental dam deep within herself. Though the day was so busy that she hardly had a moment to draw breath, Penny thought about him every second. Thought about what had existed between them, what they had shared and lost.

Most of all, she thought about the expression in his eyes when he'd accused her of aborting their child.

Naturally, he would see it like that.

It was true that she had made that horrible threat. But of course she'd never had any intention of ever carrying it out! She'd been desperate, and could think of no other threat that would stop him from following her. What had happened to her had seemed like a fateful punishment—though she'd already been sick with the brain inflammation that had almost killed her when she'd said those words.

Why had her letter never reached him? She remembered writing it.

When he didn't reply, or come to her, she'd just assumed that he had been unable to forgive what she'd done.

That his silence was his answer.

But in those agonised days after she'd been discharged from St Cyprian's, her mind had not been working properly. Perhaps she had never posted it. Perhaps even writing it had been a dream.

Certainly, Ryan had never come to her, though she had thought he would. She had been so alone, with no comfort and no hope.

He had not come, and she had moved on.

Now, as she worked busily in the banqueting hall, she reflected on how far she had travelled since those dark days. Penny had been determined that her previous life would just cease to exist, that she would make a brand-new start. And that was what she had achieved.

She was never going to be so madly unhappy again.

She looked down the high table with a critical eye. Everything looked beautiful! Each place setting was a work of art. Tara was still setting out the individual vases of flowers. Penny had made them low and wide, so they wouldn't be knocked over easily, and so that Her Worship's guests wouldn't have to peer round them to talk to each other.

The big arrangements that flanked the tables had turned out spectacular, even though the yellow gladioli she had envisioned had been toned down to a more subtle cream.

And everything went perfectly with the big centrepiece she had set up in the square formed by the four long tables. That space was to have been left empty, but at the last minute she'd had a brainwave. She was particularly proud of that.

The mayor and her private secretary bustled in now to take a last look. Her Worship was a diminutive, fiercely energetic woman who prided herself on her modern views—which was why, Penny suspected, she had chosen a newcomer to do her banquet, rather than one of the well-established, but old-fashioned, town florists.

'It's exquisite!' she enthused, patting Penny on the shoulder. 'Truly magnificent, Miss Watkins. That centrepiece is wonderful!'

'Thank you,' Penny smiled.

'A perfect autumnal note,' the mayor went on. 'The bare branches giving a home to new life, the old nurturing the new—it's quite an illustration of my mayoralty, don't you think, Daphne?'

'Absolutely, Your Worship,' the obsequious secretary chimed, her timing as perfect as a Swiss clock.

'Very original, Penny,' the mayor affirmed. 'I don't know where you creative people get all your ideas!'

Hippy Dave had helped with this one, though she could scarcely tell the mayor that; for the spectacular centrepiece was none other than the dead tree that he had brought to her workshop that morning.

Penny had attacked it with a saw borrowed from Miles Clampett, had trimmed it into a more elegant shape, then had decorated the bare branches with birds' nests—each nest containing a brood of fluffy 'chicks'—gold and silver ribbon and flower buds on the point of opening. Artfully lit with concealed highlighters, it looked stark and exciting.

'I think you can count on my patronage next year,' the mayor murmured into Penny's ear as she left. 'Well done, Penny!'

And thus, Penny smiled to herself, had the humblest of the

mayor's flock contributed to the banquet in no small way. She could almost forgive Hippy Dave.

Tara had finished setting out the posies. It was now over to the caterers and the master of ceremonies. She got ready to leave, winding her scarf around her slender throat. It had been a long, cold day, and she was looking forward to getting back to her own nest.

With a final word to Tara, she slipped out of the banquet hall—and straight into a pair of strong arms that closed possessively around her slim frame.

'Not so fast,' Ryan said.

'What are you doing here?' she gasped, looking up into his face.

'Your partner suggested I take a look at your work,' he said smoothly. 'So here I am. Now, show me what you've done.'

She disengaged herself from his arms, her face still tight from the unwelcome shock. 'It's no big deal, Ryan. Look all you want. I'm going home.'

'In a moment,' he growled, catching her hand, his fingers twining possessively through hers. 'I haven't finished with you yet.'

'Let me go!' she hissed, trying not to make a scene in front of everybody.

But he was leading her remorselessly back to the table. 'Very pretty,' he said, his grey eyes taking everything in with that swift way he had. 'Not very original, considering what you're capable of—but pretty.'

'It's a mayor's banquet, not a gathering of your glittering London friends,' she retorted, stung by his faint praise. 'They wanted pretty, not original.'

'But I see you were unable to totally squelch your creative instincts,' he said. 'There is one authentic touch. That dead-tree arrangement is inspired.'

'You like that, do you?' she said drily.

'Fledglings and flower buds on dead branches. Very symbolic.' He was wearing a jacket cut from buttery Italian leather, which fitted him like a dream and smelled delicious. She remembered it well—she'd chosen it for him in Milan, and had given it to him for a birthday. She also remembered what had happened after that—how he'd draped the jacket around her slim, naked shoulders, how he'd made love to her wearing that, and nothing else. 'There's an empty space in the entrance of Northcote Hall. An arrangement like that would go very well there.'

'I'm sorry,' she said sweetly, 'that piece is a one-off. I don't repeat myself.'

'Then think of something else,' he said, his chiselled mouth quirking in a slight smile. She had always found his mouth devastatingly attractive, with its combination of authority and sensuality. As if he'd read her thoughts like a book, he bent his dark head and kissed her on the lips. The contact was electric, and she flinched. 'Sorry,' he said ironically, 'did that hurt?'

'You're trespassing,' she warned him.

He looked her over, taking in her less than elegant work clothes with a wicked smile. 'Yes, I can see that you have "no trespassers" written all over you. Where were you skipping off to when I met you?'

'Home.'

'Good. I'll come with you.'

'You can't!' she exclaimed.

'Oh? Why not?'

'Somebody's waiting for me there!'

One eyebrow lifted disdainfully. 'That yokel who was pawing you this morning?'

'Ryan, don't do this,' she said in a low voice. 'We have nothing to say to one another.'

'On the contrary,' he said firmly. 'There's a great deal to be said on both sides. We need to talk, Penny. And we're going to talk, whether you like it or not. We can talk here, in front of the mayor and her councillors. Or we can go somewhere more private. If you won't take me to your place, then I'll take you to mine.'

One glance at his face told her he meant it. She was not prepared to let him take her off to some unknown destination, so there was no choice.

'I live around the corner,' she said, capitulating.

'And nobody is waiting for you there?'

'No.'

'Good,' he replied. 'Let's get moving.'

They walked out into the cold evening air. It was already starting to freeze again, and Penny's breath made a white cloud around her lips.

'Why are you keeping up this charade about Northcote Hall?' she asked him. 'You don't need to. Ariadne isn't here to be impressed.'

'It's no charade,' he replied.

She glanced at him sharply. 'You mean you really are staying there?'

'When I finally found out where you were hiding, I asked my people to find me a suitable rental as close to you as possible. A suburban bungalow would hardly suit my needs.'

'Oh, hardly,' she echoed with sarcasm. 'The great Ryan Wolfe in a lowly semi-detached? Perish the thought.'

'I meant only that I need to entertain. You know that. The people I work with are wealthy. They are used to things that— what was the word you used? Glitter. Northcote was the obvious choice. It's been standing empty. The owners are desperate to sell. They're renting it to me at a reasonable rate on the principle, "try before you buy".'

'The same principle you applied to me,' she said brightly as they rounded the corner. 'You're such a good businessman, my dear. And oh, goodness, it looks as if your dashing sports car is parked right outside my house. I didn't really need to tell you where I lived, did I?'

'Why did you hide from me for so long?' he asked her. 'You've wasted a year of our lives, Penny. Do you have any idea how much effort and heartache I've invested in finding you again?'

She made no reply. His silver-grey car was indeed parked outside her front door. She walked past it and opened up. Ryan followed her into the dark interior.

'Have you bought this place?' he demanded as she switched on the light in the tiny hall.

'I'm renting it from Ariadne's sister.' She knelt by the hearth and lit the fire she had prepared that morning. Flames licked swiftly around the logs. 'It's at the opposite end of the social scale from your Northcote Hall, but otherwise it's exactly the same. It's been standing empty for years and the owner is desperate to sell.'

'You've made it beautiful,' he commented, looking around at her décor.

'My usual little touches of camouflage,' she shrugged. 'When the rising damp meets the sagging roof, I'll have to move out.'

Ryan walked around the cottage, like a panther stalking round a new domain. He was looking at the paintings hanging on the walls and the sculptures that disguised ugly corners. He did not need to ask whether the art works were by her— by now he knew her style well enough.

Penny pulled off her coat and scarf and warmed her cold hands at the rising flames. 'Do you want a drink? I'm going to have a whisky on the rocks.'

It was a drink she had learned to like with Ryan. He

nodded, but made no other comment. While she poured the drinks, he was stroking the curves of a sculpture with one of his strong yet sensitive hands. 'So you got to sculpt in wood, after all,' he said.

'Yes.'

'You're very good. And your style has matured,' he said.

'I've matured,' she said.

'I can see that. You have a lot more to say.'

'To say?'

'About yourself. About what you see in the world.' He accepted the drink she offered him. 'You've become an adult.'

'How kind of you.' She didn't bother raising her glass in a toast, but took a much-needed gulp of the fiery whisky. 'We'd better sit by the fire. This house is cold and damp.'

There was one sofa, facing the fire. The glow of the flames provided a warm light. She did not switch on any more lights, not wanting him to see how bare the cottage really was, beneath the artistic touches she had lavished on it.

They sat facing each other. The rosy light that gave her smooth, pale face an alabaster glow made his look even more rugged and masculine than usual.

Or perhaps he had lost weight; his straight, Norman nose seemed more pronounced than usual, and there were shadows in the cleft of that masterfully erotic mouth.

'You look tired,' she commented.

'I've been in meetings in London all day,' he replied.

'Not that kind of tired. A deeper tiredness. Too many parties, perhaps?'

'Parties?' he repeated. 'Since you left me, my life has been nothing but work. Work, and hunting for you.'

'Well,' she said with a brittle smile, 'you obviously have plenty on your mind, Ryan. So, now that you've caught me at last, why don't you go ahead and say it?'

CHAPTER THREE

'WHERE did you go after you ran from me?' he asked.

'I went back west, to Exeter. I had some friends there.'

'And that's where you got sick?'

'Yes.'

'How did you get encephalitis?'

'They could never tell me how I caught it. It started with a terrible headache, that horrible last weekend in London. Remember how sick I was?'

'Yes,' he said grimly. 'I remember.'

'At first I thought I had bad flu. Then I started to vomit on the train. I couldn't stop. The first doctor I saw didn't recognise the symptoms, so there was a delay. I went into convulsions. By the time they got me to hospital, I was going into a coma.'

'Penny, I'm so sorry.' His face was tight. 'Why didn't you call me? I know we were fighting like tigers, but in those circumstances nothing else would have mattered. I would have run to you.'

'If it's any consolation, I remember telephoning you from the station. I think the voice-mail service picked up. I probably didn't say anything.'

'Oh, Penny. If you'd left one word—'

'I wasn't in a fit state to say much,' she shrugged. 'Don't worry about it.'

'And you say you were unconscious when you had the miscarriage?' he asked, his eyes intent.

Penny took another gulp of her whisky. 'Yes.'

'How long were you in the coma?'

'A few days. The antibiotics worked. I was very lucky. After a couple of weeks, they discharged me.'

'And then?'

She shrugged again. 'Then I got on with the rest of my life.'

'You didn't even bother to tell me your pregnancy was over.'

'I wrote to you,' she exclaimed. 'I know I did.'

'I never received a word.' His eyes were hard.

Penny shrugged. 'Maybe it got lost.'

'You're sure you wrote to me?'

'Ryan, I had just recovered from a brain inflammation. I was scarcely in my right mind. The doctors couldn't even tell me whether I was going to have permanent brain damage or not!'

'And do you have any brain damage?' he asked, watching her over the rim of his whisky glass.

'What do you care?' she retorted.

'I care a great deal. So tell me the truth.'

'I had to take anticonvulsant medication to prevent seizures. For a while.'

His penetrating grey eyes assessed her. 'For a while?'

'I didn't like the side-effects. So I stopped taking it.'

'The doctors must have been concerned, surely.'

'I didn't tell them.'

'Was that wise?'

'It was my decision. I felt much better the moment I stopped the medication. And nothing has gone wrong since.'

His gaze stayed on her for a long, assessing moment, then

moved from her to the paintings, dimly visible in the firelight. 'But the experience changed you.'

'It was a bad experience. And now I don't want to discuss it any further.'

'But I need to know everything, Penny.'

'That's too bad.'

'You have to understand,' he said evenly, 'that the last words you spoke to me were a threat to abort our child—'

'Oh, is that it?' she cut in. 'You're still wondering about that? Whether I am an evil, calculating, vicious woman, ready to commit any bloodthirsty act to get back at you.'

'Of course you aren't any of those things.'

'Then why are you so suspicious? Are you so afraid that I'm really a monster?'

'I know you're not a monster,' he said in a quiet voice. 'I wouldn't love you so much if you were.'

His words made her heart flip over like a hooked fish. 'Ryan, don't.'

'But even if you were a monster,' he went on, 'I would still love you. Helplessly and completely. I can't help loving you, you see. I was born to do it. When you love like that, it's probably not important to know anything about the one you love. It doesn't matter anyway, as you've just said. But somehow, I can't help wanting to find out.'

Her hands were trembling as she drained the whisky. 'Then I shall take great pleasure in keeping that knowledge from you,' she said in a shaky voice. 'You can just keep wondering whether I'm a liar and maybe worse.'

He had not touched the whisky with his lips yet. Now he tossed the contents of his glass into the fire with a flick of his wrist. The whisky flared into hot green and blue flames, while the ice cubes hissed and evaporated on the embers.

'Do you know what it's like to love someone, Penny?' he asked. 'I thought you did, but I must have been wrong.'

She had flinched at the blazing whisky in the hearth. The coloured flames died down now, with a hot reek of vaporised alcohol. 'You were wrong,' she said.

'It's a pity. So you don't know what it's like to desire another person with such intensity that their body becomes a whole world to you. A world whose landscape you live in, whose tastes and smells you yearn for, every waking minute. A world you can never forget, no matter how much time passes, no matter how much distance comes between, no matter how many sad things happen.'

The firelight was dancing in his eyes, and her gaze was drawn inexorably to his as he went on, his voice husky and low.

'And you don't know what it's like to ache for another person's tenderness—and not to find it. To look for a face you love so much it hurts—and not see it. To yearn for a voice that you can no longer hear.'

'That's not love,' she said unsteadily. 'That's obsession.'

'Then I'm obsessed,' he said. 'What's the difference?'

'Obsession is more dangerous,' she replied.

He shook his dark head. 'Only to me. Not to you.'

'You're dangerous to me, Ryan. That's why I had to get away from you.'

'You were too young to understand then,' he replied. He reached out and drew his fingertips slowly down her cheek. His touch was like velvet, but she shuddered in reaction. 'Now you've matured. You've been through tragedy and danger. You have grown into yourself. We're ready for each other now.'

'You're mistaken!'

His warm hand cupped the back of her neck and drew her face to his gently. Penny felt everything she had achieved over the last year start to sink into treacherous quicksand as her mouth approached his. She felt his breath on her lips, and closed her eyes.

'Ryan, I don't want this!'

'I think you do.' His mouth closed over hers.

For a moment it was as though she were drowning. And then her mind was flooded by passionate memories. They had been lovers once, such wonderful lovers.

It had been so long.

Desire rose in her with a force that could not be denied. She locked her arms around his strong neck and kissed him back, her body arching to his.

After a moment, the two of them slid to the floor in front of the fire, still locked in their embrace. The heat of the flames licked at them, igniting them still further. Ryan pulled at her blouse and Penny heard buttons snap off with the urgency of his need.

Still kissing, whispering one another's names, they undressed each other with clumsy haste. When she was naked, he pushed her onto her back and stared down at her with devouring eyes.

The blaze of the fire made tiger-stripes across his magnificent naked chest. He was like a great cat, brooding over her, and like a cat he touched her skin with his nose and drew her scent deep into his nostrils.

'You always smell so wonderful. Your skin is like rose petals.'

'A rose with thorns.' But though she uttered the warning, she was responding to him. This was insanity, worse than madness, because she was colluding with her own downfall.

He stroked the curving softness of her belly. She shuddered at his sensual caress. 'You will always be mine, Penny,' he whispered. 'Nobody else's. Mine alone.'

He kissed her nipples gently. The silky disks ruckled in his mouth, their hard tips pushing against his tongue with unabashed desire. He sucked the eager peaks, one after another, and Penny whimpered his name softly.

He gazed down at her, his eyes heavy with desire. 'I've missed you so much. I thought I had lost you forever!'

Her naked body was like alabaster in the firelight. Her hips were fuller than her narrow waist would have implied, and he stroked the curves with the fingers of an artist touching an exquisite vessel.

'Your hips were made for love, my darling,' he whispered. 'For bearing children. I'm so sorry you lost our child.'

'How could you think I would throw away my baby?' she demanded, raising herself on her elbow. 'How can you say you love me, if you think that?'

'I don't know,' he said. 'This morning I felt as though you had stabbed a dagger into my heart.'

She felt the scalding tears slide down her cheeks. They splashed onto her nipples, shining wet on her skin. 'Why did you come?'

For an answer, he sealed her mouth with his own. It was a kiss as hot as her tears, filled with passion and desire. His hands caressed her naked body, moulding the tender curves of her breasts hungrily, sliding down between her thighs to cup the nest of soft curls there.

She responded with a rush of desire that overwhelmed her.

'Have you been with anyone else since you left me?' he asked her, looking into her eyes.

'No,' she confessed. 'Have you?'

'No. So we don't need to go to the clinic for a clean bill of health before we do this...'

She kissed him to stop him saying any more.

Ryan's tongue was in her mouth, seeking her own, demanding a response. She felt his fingers encounter the melting wetness of her own desire. With gentle, expert movements of his fingers, he brought her to the very edge of her climax in no more than a few seconds. She cried out against his mouth. His own urgency matched hers. As though unable to resist any longer, he mounted her.

Penny cried out again as she felt the swollen length of his manhood between her thighs—a feeling so familiar, so thrilling, so achingly beautiful. She locked her arms around his neck and looked up into his eyes. Ryan was panting as though he had run a mile, his eyes no longer cold or hard, but glowing with passion.

She raised her hips, her thighs lifting to hold his taut, muscular waist.

The invitation was unmistakable. With a soft, purring sound, Ryan lowered his body so that his erect manhood caressed the wet petals of her sex. Penny moaned, her eyes half closing. He slid himself to and fro across the most sensitive zones of her body, arousing her unbearably.

She had been alone for so long, locked in her own misery. Now he was back, and deep inside her. Penny had not known that there was so much need in her, so much emptiness aching to be filled. So much tenderness aching to be given.

She dug her fingers into his powerful shoulders, demanding that he enter her; but it was not until she was already starting to climax that he finally thrust slowly and deeply into her body.

Ecstasy flooded her whole being. She felt herself arching against him, calling his name inarticulately. He filled her so completely, each movement bringing new waves of pleasure and fulfilment, as though her soul was stretching and expanding.

And at last he reached his own vertex and crushed her in his arms, covering her face with burning kisses.

Slowly, like leaves settling to earth after a gale, normality returned. They slid into an exhausted tangle by the fireside.

'Now that I've found you, I will never let you go.' He

pulled her head onto his chest and cradled her there, the way he used to do, long ago.

They lay in silence for a while, listening to the crackling of the flames. Then he spoke.

'I almost lost you forever, and I didn't even know. You're not safe to be out on your own. Why won't you let me cherish you for the rest of your life?'

'Because I need to live it for myself,' she said.

'I don't want to live your life for you, sweet girl. I just want to be next to you.'

'You don't. You want to swallow me up.' This was getting perilously close to the sort of arguments they'd had in London. 'And you couldn't have stopped me from getting encephalitis, anyway.'

'I would have made sure you got the best treatment, the best doctors in the world.'

'Oh, I know that, Ryan. If you could, you would have had the illness instead of me, wouldn't you?'

'Of course.'

'But I needed to have that illness for myself, my love. It was part of my life, part of my destiny, for good or for bad. To take it from me would have been to cheat me.'

'I don't agree with that,' he said. 'Avoiding misfortune is sensible. You don't have to run to it with open arms. You're too much of a pessimist.'

'A fatalist,' she corrected.

'Tell me the name of the hospital you were admitted to in Exeter.'

'Why do you want to know?'

'I would like to speak to the doctors who treated you.'

She felt icy cold, and then burning hot. 'So you can check the hospital records? To see if what I've told you about the miscarriage is true?'

There was enough strong feeling in those words to make him frown. 'Have I offended you?'

'No.' She pushed away from him and sat up, her slender body silhouetted against the firelight. 'As a matter of fact, you've just proved that you're the heartless bastard I always knew you were.'

He cocked his head at her. 'I'm the heartless one? I know I have a heart, because you broke it this morning, Penny. That was the last news I expected to hear.'

'I'm sorry, Ryan, but it was far worse for me, believe me.'

'Are you going to give me the name of the hospital?'

'So you can try and obtain my medical records? No, Ryan, I'm not. If you choose not to believe my simple word, then nothing else really matters, does it?'

'I suppose not,' he said in a strange voice.

'I think you'd better go now.' She was tying her hair back into a pony-tail, turning her face away from him so he wouldn't see the tears pouring down her cheeks.

'I'd rather stay,' he said, touching her naked shoulder.

Penny shook her head. 'You got what you wanted. Go now.'

'I want all of you,' he said, caressing her shoulder. 'I'll never be happy until I have all of you.'

'Why not be content with what you've had?' She wiped her tears away clumsily. 'You've proved I'm still a fool. You can go back to London now and forget me forever.'

He was silent for a while before answering. 'You were never this cold, this hard,' he said at last.

'As you said, I've changed. I used to be soft as putty. But not any more. I've learned to fight for myself at last.'

His arms slid around her, strong and male. 'I'll be back.' She felt him kiss the nape of her neck. 'Sweet dreams, Penny.'

Her eyes were so full of tears that the firelight was no more than a dancing orange blur that dazzled and hurt her brain. But she kept staring at it while she listened to him dress…and long after she heard the door close and his sports car drive away.

CHAPTER FOUR

SHE had given Miles Clampett the key to the workshop, and he was putting the finishing touches to the door when she arrived the next morning. Despite the bitter weather—it had snowed overnight, and the world had gone white and silent—he was whistling cheerfully.

'You look bright-eyed and bushy-tailed,' he grinned. 'You must have had some lavender under your pillow.'

'What?' she asked suspiciously. Miles was a notorious snoop, and she wondered what he was talking about.

'Us country folk,' he said, putting on a Farmer Giles accent, 'we puts lavender under our pillows to get a good night's sleep.'

'I'll remember that,' she said, stepping over a pile of shavings to get inside.

'You don't need to. I'm sure your gentleman friend knows how to ease your tensions.' He winked. 'Saw his car outside your cottage last night. And smoke coming from the chimney. Cosy.'

She didn't need Miles to remind her of last night's folly. The memory was burned into her brain as though with a red-hot branding iron. In any case, it was too early in the morning to exchange repartee with Miles.

She went inside, ignoring him.

The wisdom of last night was, at best, dubious. But however tangled her emotions were, her body evidently felt no regrets. The lingering melancholy in her system seemed to have been burned away. Her heart was beating a little faster and the blood in her veins was defying the snowy weather to make her skin flushed and glowing.

She glanced at herself in the mirror that hung in their tiny bathroom. Those roses in her cheeks had been what had caused Miles to snigger when he'd seen her. There had been a definite transformation.

She forced her thoughts away from Ryan. There was no time for introspection. She already knew that it was going to be another busy day.

The day after tomorrow was Saturday, and she had not one, but two weddings. Both were big weddings, too, meaning not just bouquets and buttonholes for the wedding parties, but churches to do as well. They would have to co-opt Tara. Luckily Tara, who was saving up to go to Australia, needed the money and never minded doing extra work.

Their business was really prospering. Hard work had never frightened Penny, and she was prepared to fight for her success.

She had no sooner started work when the phone rang. She picked it up with a hello, and was greeted by a husky, all-too-familiar voice.

'I'm sorry last night ended on a bad note. That was not the way I had planned it.'

She felt her nipples tighten in response to his voice. 'I didn't realise you'd planned it, Ryan,' she retorted, 'but I suppose I should have guessed.'

'I put that badly. I should have said, that wasn't the way I'd dreamed of it.'

'Well, I'm sorry I disappointed you.'

Ryan chuckled softly. 'Stop trying to pick holes in everything I say. Last night was wonderful. I've ached for you for so long. It was heaven to hold you, to kiss you…I only meant to apologise for offending you at the end. You took my words the wrong way.'

'Did I?'

'Penny, you still don't understand me. Sometimes I wonder if you ever will.'

'You're right,' she replied. 'I don't understand you, Ryan. I don't understand why you've come looking for me. The fact that you've taken the trouble to track me down shows that you don't understand me, either. Or that you simply don't care.'

His voice softened. 'Wasn't last night wonderful for you? I know it was. And I know that this morning your blood is tingling, just like mine. You feel alive for the first time since you left me. Isn't that true?'

She felt an awkward resentment at his accuracy. 'Sex is a completely different thing from love. Sex can be wonderful between total strangers.'

'Oh?' There was a different note in his voice now. 'You know this from experience?'

'That doesn't concern you,' she replied smartly. 'I'm very busy, Ryan. Was there anything else?'

'I want to see you tomorrow night.'

'No!'

'I'm back in London,' he went on, ignoring her protest. 'I have business here until tomorrow. I want you to have dinner with me at Northcote tomorrow night. You can advise me on how to furnish the place—it's still empty.'

'I keep telling you, but you won't listen—we have nothing to say to each other!'

'And I have some things of yours,' he concluded smoothly. 'When you ran out on me in London, you left half your stuff behind. Photographs of your parents, letters, the jewellery I gave you.'

'I don't want the jewellery,' she assured him. 'Please take it back.'

'Well, there's a beautiful Adam fireplace at Northcote,' he said. 'I'll make a nice big blaze, and throw everything on it, shall I?'

'No! I want the photographs!'

'Then come and get them,' he said succinctly. 'Tomorrow night at seven.'

'Ryan—'

The line had clicked dead in her ear.

She slammed the phone down with a growl of frustration.

'So who is he?' Miles Clampett asked through a mouthful of nails. He had sauntered in, and was leaning against the door jamb with his usual smirk. 'An old flame, obviously.'

'Have you been eavesdropping?' she demanded.

'Not half,' he admitted, taking the nails out of his mouth. 'But then, you were shouting so loud I could hear you in the mews. Come on, Penny, we're old friends. Who is he?'

'His name's Ryan Wolfe,' she said with a sigh. 'I knew him in London.'

'What's he do for a living? Rob banks?'

'More or less. But not at gun-point. He's a financier in the movie business. He puts together projects for films.'

Miles looked impressed. 'What kind of films?'

'Anything that interests him. Short films, long films, documentaries, serious films, commercial blockbusters. Whatever he thinks is going to work. He brings together consortiums of investors and introduces them to the creative people.'

Miles whistled. 'Looks like he's successful.'

She shrugged. 'He's very good at what he does. Not all his projects make money. Sometimes he does things because he believes in the talent of the people involved, even though he knows it won't be a huge commercial success. But generally, he comes out of each project considerably ahead of the game.'

Miles was examining the nails in his hand. 'And you and him? You had a big scene together in London?'

'We knew each other.'

'That much is obvious, darling. In the biblical sense, and all other senses. So what went wrong between two such beautiful people?'

'None of your business!'

'Touchy, touchy.'

'It's over now,' she replied tersely. 'That's all that matters.'

'Might be over for you,' Miles grinned, 'but it doesn't look as if it's over for him!'

'I have to work now,' she said, turning away.

'So you don't want him? But he wants you? Interesting situation!'

'Go away, Miles,' she said firmly.

'Oh, I'm going,' Miles said. 'My work here is done, earthling. I'll be sending you my bill when I can think of a figure exorbitant enough.'

'Did you fix the door properly?' Penny asked suspiciously.

'Your back door is better nor it ever was,' Miles confirmed. 'Hope it keeps away the big, bad wolf, little piggy.'

So what went wrong between two such beautiful people?

Miles's not-so-innocent question echoed in her mind as Penny drove cautiously along the snowy lanes that led to Northcote Hall. There was no way she could have answered Miles easily. To understand, you would have to have known so much about her life—and about the sort of person she had been when she had first met Ryan Wolfe.

About the sort of person he had been when he'd first burst into her life.

He'd been like a god to her then. Like the rising sun, turning the darkness into dazzling light and heat.

But then, she had been so young.

Just twenty-one years old.

Ryan had been twenty-nine, and the eight years that separated them had made a very wide gulf between them. He was already highly successful, a man of money and influence—she was a university drop-out with little more than a gift for décor.

He was at the centre of a glittering world of celebrities and big shots; she was alone and painfully shy.

He was a man to whom conquering beautiful women came ridiculously easy. She was a woman still broken-hearted and withdrawn after a love affair that had started badly and ended much worse.

She was confused and uncertain, not knowing what to do with her young life. Ryan was so certain of everything he did, driving down the rails of life like a locomotive, pulling everything and everyone behind his power and authority.

When they came together, it had been no contest.

They met on the set of a movie being shot in a beautiful but run-down Georgian house in Hampstead. It was a low-budget art movie, based on a Victorian novel. The minimal finances meant that the producers were cutting costs wherever they could, so Penny, fresh in town and just about willing to work for food, had been lucky enough to get the job of doing the flowers.

She'd done them so brilliantly that by the time they were shooting the principal scenes, she was doing far more than just the flowers. She was essential to every shot, adding the inspired touches that brought the sets to life. They'd taken to consulting her on almost every detail of the backgrounds. And she, thirsty for knowledge, was drinking in the mysteries of film-making in great gulps.

Ryan Wolfe walked onto the set one morning to see how his baby was doing—all his films were his 'babies'—took one look at her, and decided there and then that she was his.

That was so typical of his certainty, his arrogance. Turning her into one of his projects. His latest 'baby'.

But things were edgy between them right from the start. Being swept off her feet by an older man was exactly what Penny didn't want to happen to her right then.

She had been there, done that.

Penny told Ryan the reason for her dropping out of university in the second year of her fine arts degree—her doomed love affair with the much older lecturer which had made her so unhappy. How it had ended by wrecking her happiness, her studies and her life.

Ryan seemed to listen as she told him about Tom, who had exploited the innocence and trust of his best and prettiest student—as he'd done with other brilliant and pretty students before her.

Ryan seemed to listen, yes. Then he kissed her and told her to forget Tom, that it was all over, that she was starting a new life now.

Problem solved.

He never understood that what Tom had done to her had left Penny very vulnerable. That there was a very real danger he would be a second Tom in her life. That he would trap her in just the same way. Despite all those warnings, he couldn't leave her alone.

He wanted her so much.

So much that he was unable to give her what she so desperately needed—time. Time to get over Tom, to take a look at her life, time to consider the decisions she needed to take.

He swept all her objections aside. To all her pleadings, Ryan had the same answer—he knew best.

Lucky Ryan, Penny thought bitterly as she drove through the wintry landscape. It must be so pleasant to know what was best for other people. It made life so simple. To be so free of self-doubt that the tangled lives of others were nothing more than simple puzzles to be solved with a few clever moves!

But when she'd learned that she was expecting his baby, that she was going to become a mother in a few months, she'd known there was no way to solve that particular puzzle.

It was the last straw.

Desperate to escape, to be alone with herself and look into her own heart, she told Ryan she was leaving.

Ryan, overjoyed at the news that he was going to have a real baby at last, that his beloved was going to bear him a child, was flabbergasted.

Why did she want to leave him now? Now, when their love was bearing such wonderful fruit? Now, when she was going to need him more than ever?

Because she felt that her life was closing around her before it had even begun. Because she was in a trap between Ryan and her baby, with no escape at either end.

The arguments raged. Until, driven by desperation, she made that terrible threat. He was stunned just long enough for her to make her escape—and disappear from his life forever.

She'd never dreamed that biology would turn her over-heated words into a tragic reality.

It was snowing lightly as she drove to Northcote. The headlights of her little delivery van shimmered on the snowbound roads. There was no traffic except the occasional owl sweeping through the bare trees. The high stone wall to her right meant that she was already driving along the boundary of Northcote Hall.

In its heyday, Penny knew that Northcote had been one of the finest country houses in this part of Kent, with gardens designed by Capability Brown and architectural details by Robert Adam.

In recent years, the house had stood empty. The owners, finding it too expensive to maintain, had put it on the market. They had modernised the house, and it was in good condition, but almost all of its once famous furnishings had been sold off, leaving the house bare. It was in need of a major refurnishing that would depend on finding a wealthy purchaser.

Though Ryan Wolfe was probably easily rich enough to buy the grand old place and fill it with the beautiful furniture and art it deserved, she somehow doubted whether he was serious about that.

Ryan was too restless, too much a lover of new things and adventures, to want to be tied to a life-long project like Northcote.

She reached the gates now and drove up the tree-lined avenue to the house. She would have to postpone her memories and meditations until after her drink with Ryan. Her stomach was tightening with nerves, and she felt her mouth start to dry up.

It added to her dismay to see that there were two other cars parked beside Ryan's outside the Palladian entrance. He had not warned her that he had invited guests, people from the movie world, by the look of their expensive cars.

She sat clutching the wheel with sweating hands, her heart pounding, poised to flee like a bird. She did not want to face this. Not tonight, not when Ryan's re-entry in her life had shaken her up so much.

But then a dark figure loomed up next to her van, and it was too late to flee.

She lowered her window slowly. Ryan leaned down, his handsome face speckled with snowflakes, and smiled at her. 'I'm glad you came,' he said softly.

'You wretch,' she retorted. 'You didn't tell me there would be anyone else.'

'They're leaving in a short while,' he told her. 'In any case, you know them both, Penny. And they're dying to see you. Switch off your engine and come in.'

CHAPTER FIVE

His warm hand was on the small of her back as he ushered her into the house.

Her gaze was drawn upwards to the great sweep of the moulded ceiling, and the marble staircase that led to the upper floor. The emptiness of the house somehow added to its grandeur, giving it a theatrical feel that was entirely at one with Ryan's larger-than-life presence.

'Glorious, isn't it?' he commented. 'It's big, but it has such noble proportions, you don't notice the size.'

'It suits you,' she said. She looked at him. He was not so unkempt-looking as he had been a few days ago. His dark hair had been neatly trimmed and his face was more relaxed. He'd shaved, and he smelled of some delicious cologne. He was wearing a dark suit with a dark grey polo-neck. As always, in elegant clothes he looked utterly stunning.

He helped her out of her coat, underneath which she was wearing jeans, boots and a white embroidered blouse. It was hardly the smartest outfit she possessed.

'I would have dressed to meet company if you'd warned me, Ryan.'

'It's not a formal occasion.' Ryan's deep eyes, with their thick black fringe of lashes, surveyed her up and down. 'And you look beautiful, darling girl.' He hung her coat under the stairs, then took her arm. 'Come.'

The room he led her to was evidently a library or study, with beautiful linenfold panelling. But the shelves were bare of books and the room contained only some well-worn leather armchairs, drawn up around the fire that burned brightly in the hearth.

As she walked into the room Dame Lucinda Strong rose from her chair, spreading her arms. 'Penny! Dear heart! How wonderful to see you again!'

It was an embrace which brought a lump to Penny's throat. The celebrated actress, who was one of Ryan's close friends, had been very kind to Penny, and seeing her was almost like seeing her dead mother again. Lucinda was already in middle age, but her face was filled with a glow of motherly beauty.

Waiting in line to hug her was David Warlock, a distinguished film producer known for his powerful movies about love, who rarely appeared in public lately.

'Welcome back, precious,' he said, squeezing her tight. 'We all missed you.'

'We did indeed,' Lucinda smiled, as Ryan seated Penny between them and put a glass of champagne into her hand.

'I've just been here, working,' she said awkwardly.

'You're more beautiful than ever,' David Warlock told her in his quiet way. 'It's good to have you back.' He patted her hand. On the set, he had one of the most commanding presences in the movies, but his off-set manner was far gentler, often tinged with unexpected melancholy. With his mane of silver hair and his aquiline face, David reminded Penny of an ancient druid. But she knew he was in almost total retirement these days, and she wondered what could have brought him out of his Celtic sanctuary.

These two people, Penny knew, belonged to Ryan's inner

circle. They were very different from each other in style. The reclusiveness of David Warlock, who lived in isolation on the west coast of Ireland nowadays, contrasted with Lucinda Strong's extrovert manner, very much the *grande dame* of the theatre.

But they had something in common. Though they made their living in a world where insincerity was all too common, they were rock-solid. Though both had achieved great success, there was not a false note or a fake smile around this fireplace.

Ryan, she quickly realised, was raising funds for a movie to be directed by David Warlock, his first film in years. He had come across a script called *The Other Side*, which he described as 'the most original thing I've read in years', the story of a passionate love affair between a young man and an older woman. None of the studios had been interested so far. But David Warlock loved the script, Lucinda Strong was intrigued by the lead role, and Ryan was doing his best to encourage them both.

'It's been ages since you've done anything romantic, Lucinda,' he pointed out. 'Not since *Autumn in Shanghai*.'

'That's because I'm an old lady now, sweetheart,' she said. 'I play batty grandmothers and wicked witches these days, that's all I'm fit for.' But her eyes were sparkling, and the famous smile was hovering on her lips.

'Are you fishing for compliments?' Ryan sighed. 'You're a great beauty, and you know it. But that's hardly the point. You're the only actress with the emotional range to do this part justice.'

'But all those bedroom scenes,' Lucinda protested. 'People don't want to see the Nurse in bed with Romeo. It's not appealing.'

There was a grunt of protest from David Warlock.

'*The Other Side* is a poignant story about an unusual and beautiful love affair,' David said in his soft voice. 'Only an actress with a beautiful soul could play Tamara.'

Lucinda turned to Penny, who was smiling quietly as she listened to the debate. 'What do you think, Penny Bun?' It was her pet name for the younger woman. 'Actresses should stop playing sexy roles when they're no longer young, don't you agree?'

'I haven't read the script,' Penny said, 'but love doesn't have an age limit. Nor does sex. There just aren't any barriers. And you are such a powerful actress that you make all your roles unforgettable.'

'The flattery apart,' Lucinda smiled, 'do you really think the public want to see a grey-haired Juliet?'

'I think if Romeo and Juliet had met in a retirement home, they would have fallen in love just as passionately.'

The others, who had been listening, agreed. David nodded approval. 'Bravo. Well said, Penny.'

Snow was now starting to fall heavily again. The roads would soon be impassable. It was time for the little meeting to break up.

Lucinda turned to Penny as they walked out, and said in a low voice, 'It's so wonderful to see you and Ryan together again, Penny. He's been lost without you. We were all quite worried about him this last year. He's just started to look his old self again in the past few days.'

Penny looked into the wise eyes of the legendary actress. 'We're not exactly together again, Lucinda.'

'You're together tonight, at any rate. You and Ryan make one of the most perfect matches I've ever seen.'

She grimaced. 'Appearances can be deceptive. We're very different people.'

'Haven't you just been telling me that there are no barriers to love?' Lucinda said with a smile.

'That's true,' Penny agreed. 'But some kinds of love consume people. They don't leave any room for you to be yourself.'

'I think you will always be yourself,' Lucinda commented. 'But I have a different outlook, in any case. I think people only become themselves when they are truly in love.'

Penny knew that Lucinda had lost her husband, and she could not think of anything to reply except, 'I'm so sorry, Lucinda.'

'I'm still in love with him,' Lucinda replied lightly. 'I always will be. It's incurable, you know.'

'Is it because you lost Bill that you're hesitant about this part?' Penny asked.

'Partly,' Lucinda admitted.

'Perhaps you could do it for him,' Penny said softly. 'A tribute to him?'

Lucinda smiled wryly. 'You and Ryan are cut from the same cloth, my dear. Well, I'll think about it. Now, tell me something—why did you leave Ryan?'

'It all got too much for me,' Penny replied, not knowing any other way to put it.

'Ryan's lifestyle?'

'No...I got used to the jet-setting, the celebrities, the pace. It was just Ryan himself. He gave me no space.'

'The important thing is that you've let Ryan back into your life.'

'I'm doing my best to get him out of my life again!'

'Ryan is a very special man,' Lucinda said gently. 'He's a kind of magician. He brings people together, people who seem to have nothing in common, and then wonderful things happen. I don't think he's the domineering monster you think he is. He's just very sure of himself. And I know he's very sure that he's the right man for you.'

The words echoed what Ryan had said to her, and Penny shook her head slightly. 'He can't take that decision for me.'

'Oh, I know! I suspect that you still love Ryan, and that you always will. He just has to learn to give you more space.'

Penny caught Ryan's bright grey eyes on her. He smiled in a way that always made her heart turn over in her breast. No doubt he was pleased she had done her bit towards persuading Lucinda Strong to take the role.

Lucinda had caught the glance between Ryan and Penny. 'He adores you, Penny,' she said gently.

'In his way, I suppose he does. You see, I had a bad experience when I was at university. I never had a chance to get over that. Ryan blew into my life like a tempest. Everything was too much, Lucinda. Even his love. He loves me too much, pushes me too much, dominates me too much. My soul wasn't my own any more. And then—' She was about to mention her pregnancy, but that was too painful a topic to bring up, and she stopped short.

'And then something happened?' Lucinda asked, looking at Penny with shrewd eyes. 'Something you don't want to talk about?'

'I had some bad times,' she said with an effort. 'I was sick for a while, and…'

Lucinda put an arm around her shoulders. 'I know. Ryan told me you had a bad time in Exeter. I'm sorry.'

Penny froze. 'He told you about Exeter?'

'He didn't tell me anything specific,' Lucinda smiled. 'He just said you had been ill there. The doctors told him you almost died.'

She felt even colder. 'The doctors?'

'He went up to the hospital where you were treated, a couple of days ago. I thought you knew.' Lucinda's face clouded as she saw Penny's expression of horror. 'Oh, dear. Perhaps I shouldn't have told you that!'

Penny forced a facsimile of a smile onto her icy lips. 'No, it's all right. So that's where he went. To Exeter. Not London.'

'Penny, I shouldn't have spoken. Please forgive me.'

'There's nothing to forgive,' Penny said brightly. 'Believe me, Lucinda, I would much rather have known.'

Watching the tail-lights of the last car receding into the whirling clouds of snow, with Ryan's arm tight around her waist, Penny was rigid with cold anger.

'I'm so proud of you,' Ryan said, kissing her neck. 'You make everybody love you.'

'I don't set out to do that. And it wasn't very fair to spring that on me.'

'I needed to talk to Lucinda and David. I'm excited about this project. And you were perfect,' he said.

'I'm always perfect, aren't I?' she said.

'Yes, as a matter of fact, you are,' he replied, smiling. 'Are you angry with me about something?'

'You could say that.'

He led her in, out of the cold. 'What is it?' he asked, looking intently down at her.

'I hear you took a little trip to Exeter,' she said in a taut voice. 'A fact-finding mission, was it? Gathering background for a new film, perhaps?'

His face seemed to close. 'Lucinda told you.'

'Yes. Mind you, I should have guessed, shouldn't I? I should be used to your devious ways by now. So what did you do? Did you walk into St Cyprian's disguised as a doctor in green scrubs, and demand my medical records? Or did you merely have to seduce some starry-eyed filing clerk?'

'I did not try to get access to your medical records,' he said quietly.

'Oh, tell your lies to someone else,' she retorted.

'They wouldn't have shown them to me, even if I had asked for them,' he went on. 'And I would never have asked.'

'Ryan, you believe I'm your property. You think you own

me, and have the right to take every decision for me.' She was panting with anger as she spat the words at him. 'So nothing you do surprises me any more. What did you do? Get some specialist friend of yours to put in the request? Pull my file so you could satisfy yourself as to whether I deliberately aborted your child?'

'It is hateful to hear those words come out of your mouth,' he said, the coldness of his tone matching her heat now.

'It doesn't really matter.' Penny's eyes were dark violet, as they often were when she was deeply upset. His, by contrast, were icy grey. Their gazes locked. 'The mere fact that you went to St Cyprian's, prying and snooping, shows you for what you are.'

His mouth, normally so sensual, was a grim line. 'And what am I?'

'Someone so concerned about himself that he has no feeling for others. You went there because you didn't believe what I told you. You wanted to prove that I lied to you, that my sickness never happened, that I jettisoned that baby to spite you.'

He was obviously controlling his temper with an effort. 'That's not true. I went to St Cyprian's because of you. Because of something you said.'

'I hope you satisfied your curiosity,' she said savagely. 'I hope it was worth it. Because I'm going to contact St Cyprian's, too. And if I find out that they released my medical records to you, I'm going to let loose the biggest scandal you've ever seen. I'm going to drag them—and you—through the courts and the newspapers and anyone else who will listen. I don't care what it costs me. But I'll make you sorry! Thank you for a lovely evening, Ryan. Goodbye.'

She hurried out of the house, ducking her head against the blizzard of snowflakes.

She heard him calling after her, but she flung open the door of her little van and jumped inside. She was so angry that her breath was coming raggedly through clenched teeth.

Penny started the engine and drove off down the drive, fast, her wheels spinning in the loose snow.

Snow was falling so thickly that her windscreen wipers could not cope with it, and merely smeared the crystals in icy sheets on the glass. It was very cold in the car. Her breath was clouding around her mouth and nose.

She reached the tall stone gateposts and drove out onto the road. If she had left with the others, instead of staying to give Ryan a piece of her mind, she would at least have been able to follow their tail-lights. As it was, the road was pitch-black, her headlights no more than a diffuse dazzle in the whirling flakes of snow. She felt very lonely.

Damn him, she thought in fresh outrage. How dare he? She had meant every word of her threat. If he had somehow in-veigled the hospital into releasing her records, she would make them—and him—pay dearly.

To speak of love! To tell her he adored her! And then to snoop into her most private details, looking for evidence that she had told a horrible lie—her blood was boiling.

Cursing, she skidded along the narrow road. It was like driving through an unlit tunnel. Then she sighed with relief. She knew where she was, at last. The road dipped steeply down here to cross Fotheringham Bridge. She steered cau-tiously over the narrow stone bridge, then accelerated hard to get up the hill on the other side of the stream.

The van responded with a surge of power.

And then the rear wheels were spinning out of control, and the car began to turn on its own axis.

'Oh, no!' she heard herself say.

She'd had no idea her little van could spin so fast.

It went completely around, once, twice, and on the third time it shot backwards through a hedge. Clinging to the steering wheel, Penny bounced in her seat wretchedly as she heard twigs snapping all around the car.

Her rearwards progress ended with a jolt as the back of the van thumped into a ditch of some kind. She revved the engine desperately, but her wheels just whirled uselessly in the slush.

She was well and truly stuck.

Penny thumped the steering wheel in frustration. What an idiot. She should have remembered that the van was much more powerful than previous cars she'd driven. Now, here she was, stuck in a hedge in the middle of a snowstorm.

She recalled the advice she had been given. If you're stuck in the snow, don't leave the car. Keep the engine running, keep warm, wait for help.

But the prospect of sitting in the van all night, alone with her misery, was not an attractive one.

She was already starting to shiver.

And then, to her joy, headlights glimmered in the distance. Help was at hand!

Wrapping her coat around her cold body, she pulled herself out of the car and stood at the roadside, her eyes squinting against the swirling snowflakes. The lights grew brighter and brighter until, with a rumble, a big four-wheel-drive car came slowly up from the bridge.

She waved urgently, dazzled by the headlights.

To her intense joy, the Land Cruiser ground to a halt beside her, gleaming and luxurious-looking. She was filled with a mixture of relief that she had been saved and embarrassment that she had done something so foolish.

'Thank you so much for stopping,' she called.

A tall figure got out of the Land Cruiser.

'It's a pleasure,' said Ryan Wolfe. 'I was just wondering which particular ditch I would find you in.'

CHAPTER SIX

SHE was a very much more subdued Penny as he ushered her back into the hallway of Northcote.

'Don't worry,' he said, 'your van will be safe there until tomorrow. It doesn't look as though there's too much damage. I'll pull it out of the hedge in the daylight with the Land Cruiser and you'll probably be able to drive it home.'

'Thanks for coming to my rescue,' she said morosely. She was fully expecting that he would gloat over her humiliation.

'I thought you might get into trouble,' he said gently. 'You shot off out of here like a scalded cat. Fresh snow is very treacherous. That's why I followed you in the Land Cruiser. I'm just relieved you didn't break your beautiful neck.'

'Me, too,' she admitted.

He helped her take off her coat. 'You're freezing. I've got a fire upstairs. And your photos and things are there, too. Come upstairs, I'll give them to you.'

The great, empty house was silent, yet it seemed warm and welcoming as she went up the staircase with Ryan. He had chosen for his own one of the bedrooms that looked out over the lawns behind the house. It was a big room with a large four-poster bed in the middle. A fire had been burning in the grate, and had now burned down to a pile of glowing logs.

'Sorry it's a little cold in here,' he said, putting two more logs on the fire. 'I think a new heating system will be the first thing I install when I buy the house.'

'You're really going ahead and buying it?' she asked.

'I think so. I suppose I'll have to start looking for some staff to run the place soon.'

'When you talked about buying Northcote, I thought you were just trying to pull the wool over Ariadne's eyes. I didn't for a moment think you were serious!'

'Why not?' he asked.

'Well—for one thing, this is a grand mansion. The owners must want a fortune for it!'

'Money is one thing I have plenty of,' he said. 'You know that.'

'Well, for another, you're not exactly the domesticated type.'

Ryan cocked his head at her quizzically. 'Now, what on earth do you mean by that?'

'Well…you have the flat in London.' She thought of that beautiful apartment in Knightsbridge, with its Swedish furnishings and starkly modern décor, where she had been so unhappy. 'You always said that was all you needed. Low-maintenance, minimal upkeep, lock the door and fly to Mexico at the drop of a hat if you needed. It's a very big step from that to this.'

'A very big step,' he agreed. 'But you see, my love, I've taken some very big steps since we parted. I've changed and matured, just as you have.' He lifted a leather box onto the four-poster and opened it. 'Here are your things. Everything's all mixed up. You'd better sort through it.'

Penny sat on the bed and looked into the box. It was like looking into a kaleidoscope of her own life, and for a moment she felt her head spin.

Here were old photographs of her parents. Her father, dashing in tennis kit. Her mother, pretty and carefree. Photographs of herself as a child, chubby and adorable in pigtails. Then photographs of her mother with Aubrey, her stepfather, after her father's early death, her stepfather's face kindly and smiling, her mother's face tranquil, but permanently marked by the grief she had passed through.

There were photos from her own adolescence and early adulthood, the chubby little girl turning into a slender beauty with a steady gaze and an expressive mouth. Herself at nineteen, already under the spell of Tom, the professor who had seduced her, her eyes already darkening with pain.

There were other mementoes, too, beads and rings and theatre tickets and concert passes.

And a blue velvet box that Ryan opened.

'Remember this?' he said, sitting beside her. He took the ruby necklace out. In the firelight, the stones glittered with deep crimson lights. She stared at the necklace. He had bought it for her the week she'd learned she was unquestionably pregnant, a gift so expensive that it had made her feel even more panic, even more alarm. As though those exquisite Burmese stones were links in a chain that was winding ever more tightly around her.

'Put it on,' he murmured, opening the clasp.

'I don't want it.'

'Just for a moment. I don't think you wore this more than once.'

'You should sell it. It's much too valuable to keep lying around.'

'I will never sell it. It belongs to you, darling.' He placed the necklace round her neck. His beautiful grey eyes looked deep into hers as he reached around the back of her neck to fasten the clasp. 'There.'

Penny looked down. The strands of rubies were like drops of blood, she thought, frozen in time. They lay against her blouse, glowing vividly.

'It's too long for that shirt,' he said quietly. 'Let me unfasten these buttons.'

His strong fingers were sure and deft as they unbuttoned her blouse, revealing the milky smoothness of her throat. He opened the lapels of the blouse. She wore a pale gold bra beneath it, the full curves of her breasts cupped in aureate lace.

'There,' he said huskily. 'That's better.'

Against her pale skin, the rubies took on a new note. No longer like blood, they had become crystals of fire whose hot, sensual colour belied their cool caress on her bosom.

'You're so lovely,' Ryan whispered. He bent to press his face to the scented hollow between her breasts, a place on her body he had always loved to kiss.

His touch made her shudder again, and she could not prevent her eyes from closing, or her head from going back— any more than she could prevent her arms from sliding round his strong neck, or her fingers from invading the crisp, dark curls of his hair.

Then she made a valiant effort to draw her blouse closed again. 'I should go now,' she said.

'Not just yet.' His tone was halfway between a lover's plea and a tyrant's command. 'Stay with me a while.'

'It's late.'

'I've missed you so, Penny.' His breath was warm against her skin. He held her as tenderly as though she were a faun that might start away at the slightest noise. 'Have you missed me?'

Her mouth was dry. 'At first…'

'At first?' he prompted, when her words dried up.

Penny closed her eyes. 'Nothing.' It would serve no purpose to tell him how desolate she had been in those terrible weeks after she had been discharged from St Cyprian's, how she had longed for his strength and comfort.

Later, she had been glad that he hadn't come to her then.

She would certainly have ended up in the velvet prison she'd taken such pains to escape from!

It was just as well that he had never received her letter. Some kindly fate had been looking after her.

'Nothing,' she repeated.

Ryan kissed her throat, inhaling the scent of her skin and her perfume. She ran her hands across his shoulders, feeling their power and breadth. Then, with the last of her strength, she tried to push him away.

'Stay,' he whispered.

'You must have a guest room. Let me go to it!'

'But we're here now,' he said, his lips brushing the delicate skin under her chin. 'We've got all night and all of tomorrow.' He kissed the corners of her mouth. 'Stay with me. You don't want to be alone tonight, and nor do I.'

She had no answer to that. His palms slid possessively up her back, his fingers unhooking her bra. The golden cups dropped forward, releasing her high, proud breasts. Her nipples, exquisitely sensitive to his proximity, were already rising eagerly.

Ryan kissed them lingeringly. 'They're magic,' he said with a secret smile at her. 'They turn from pink satin to pink corduroy.'

She had to smile in return. 'Practical magic.'

And then she allowed him to draw her down into his arms.

She had forgotten—or had willingly hidden the memory—of how glorious his lovemaking could be.

His body was beautiful, and he used it uninhibitedly to give and take pleasure. His thirst for her was unquenchable. At times they slept, curled up against one another's bodies, but soon she would drift back into wakefulness, stirred by his kisses into fresh desire, fresh need.

The snow whirled against the window-panes with no sign

of stopping. The huge four-poster was a world, a universe for them alone. She watched, drugged with pleasure, as Ryan rose to put more logs on the fire. Silhouetted against the amber glow of the flames, he was like a fire god from some ancient legend, whose touch brought burning pleasure that never died away.

He came back to her and sat beside her on the bed, stroking her breasts so that she purred like a contented cat.

'Were you telling me the truth when you said you hadn't been with anyone since you left me?' he asked.

'Of course. Why would I lie to you?'

'I'm just jealous.'

'You don't need to be,' she said, smiling up at him.

'Do I give you pleasure?'

'If you don't know that you do, you must be blind and deaf!'

Ryan laughed. 'Then why…?'

'Why what?'

'Why do you keep running away from me?'

'I'm sure narcotics must be very nice, too, but I would run from them as well, Ryan.'

'I'm not very flattered to be compared to a dangerous drug.'

'You ought to be put on a schedule and used only in emergencies,' she retorted. 'You shouldn't be available over the counter.'

'I'm not available over any counter that I know of,' he said, his eyebrows coming down. 'I'm only available to you.'

His caressing hands had found their way to her loins, and her thighs parted languorously to allow him access. 'Yes,' she whispered, 'but it's like having opium on prescription. It's too tempting.' She covered her face with her hands.

Ryan kissed her fingers. 'What's the matter?'

'I don't know why I can't resist you, Ryan,' she said in a stifled voice. 'I sometimes believe you are a dangerous drug, and that I will never manage to get free of you.'

He sighed. 'I can only tell you that I have never loved like this before, Penny, and that I never will love like this again. You are the woman of my dreams, the great love of my life. From the moment I saw you on that film set, I had to have you. And when you left me, it was as though somebody turned out all the lights and left me in the darkness.'

'Why did you go to Exeter?' she choked. 'Why don't you trust me, if you love me so much?'

'Penny, it is you who won't trust me. I did not go to St Cyprian's to pry into the circumstances of your miscarriage. I went because you told me you were on anticonvulsant medication, and that you stopped taking it without consulting the doctors.'

Penny uncovered her face slowly and glared at him. 'What business is that of yours?'

Ryan sighed. 'You know very well that after encephalitis, there are dangers. When you told me you'd stopped taking the medication, I was very concerned. I wanted to know what the consequences might be. For your sake.'

'That doesn't excuse your prying!'

'Perhaps not. The fact is, you should not have stopped taking the medication. I spoke to the neurologist who treated you in Exeter, Ellis Brent-Jones. He was very concerned about you. You were supposed to go back to him for regular check-ups. You've never been to see him.'

'I've been fit and well. That's more important than check-ups with old Brent-Jones.'

'Oh, you little idiot.' He paused, and was silent for a while, gently stroking the swathes of her rich auburn hair. At last he continued. 'You are like a drug to me, too.'

'That's what I keep saying. We're bad for each other!'

'Hmm. I wouldn't agree with that.' He kissed her belly tenderly, then caressed her thighs with his lips. 'But after you left, I realised something—that I know so little about you. Our life together in London was so full. There was so much work to be done, so much travelling, so many other people in our lives, that we never had time to communicate. When we were together, we made love. And then fell into an exhausted sleep. We've never talked.'

'You never wanted to listen,' she said with asperity.

'I'm listening now.'

'You can't listen with your mouth down there,' she said as he nuzzled between her thighs again, hungry to taste her all over again.

'I don't listen with my mouth,' he said, licking the honeyed bud of her desire.

She moaned. 'It's too late for talking, in any case,' she whispered. 'We've lost everything.'

Ryan raised his head. His beautiful grey eyes met hers. 'No,' he said gently. 'We haven't lost everything.'

'Well, we can't carry on like this,' she said.

Ryan raised himself on his elbows to study her face. 'What do you mean by that?' he asked.

'You said you know nothing about me, and that's true. You think you understand me, but there are things about me that you've never even begun to grasp.'

'Such as?' he asked.

'Such as what Tom did to me,' she said. 'Such as what frightens me about you. What makes me panic, even when we're at our happiest.'

'Tell me, then. Tell me now, Penny, I'm listening.'

'It's too late for any of that.'

His face was concentrated. 'What do you want, Penny?'

She swallowed. 'I want you to leave me alone.'

'Don't ask me that,' he said. 'I spent a year without you.'

'If you buy this house,' she said, 'I'll run away again.'

'Penny—'

'I promise you I will,' she said. 'You can spend what you like on Northcote Hall. I'll close up the shop and go somewhere else, somewhere you'll never find me!'

'How can you talk like that when we've just made such beautiful love?' he demanded.

'Because I need time, Ryan!'

'You've had a whole year,' he pointed out. 'If you haven't worked out your own mind in that time, you never will.'

'I certainly never will while you are near me.'

'Don't ask me to leave you again,' he repeated. He was obviously taking her threat seriously. His eyes were intent. 'But I'm prepared to compromise.'

'What do you mean?' she asked suspiciously.

'I'll give you space. Time. I'll learn about you, about who you are and what you need. And I won't crowd you while I'm learning.'

'What does that mean?'

'If you stay here, I'll agree to only see you when you want me. On your terms.'

'No unannounced visits?'

'Only by appointment,' he smiled.

'I don't believe you,' she said mistrustfully.

'If you want, I'll ask permission before each and every meeting. And if you say no, I'll stay away. But you have to promise me three things.'

'What are they?' she asked.

'Firstly, that you will help me decorate this house. Help me choose furnishings, furniture, décor, art. I need your sense of style, your taste. Your knowledge of art history. And that also means doing my parties. At least one a week.'

'I'm not stupid. If I agree to that,' she pointed out briskly, 'then we'll be thrown together all the time.'

'Not necessarily. I have my work, as always. I'll give you a free hand. We need only meet on a professional basis. Unless you say otherwise. I'll pay you whatever you ask.'

Penny studied his face. 'Whatever I ask?'

'I'm very generous, you know that. And I'm sure you need the business.'

'What if you don't approve of my taste?'

Ryan smiled, stroking her cheek. 'You have the most exquisite taste I know of. You can do everything exactly as you wish. I won't interfere. Effectively, you'll be mistress of this house.'

'With a budget?'

'We'll put it on a business footing,' he assured her. 'You can have a company cheque-book of your own.'

'What are the other things I have to promise?'

'Another is that you have to go back to St Cyprian's for that check-up. And do it soon.'

'And the third?'

'The third is this,' he said simply, kissing the triangle of curls at her loins. 'That you'll be faithful to me. That when you need love, you will come to me.'

'Can I have a company cheque-book for that, too?'

He grinned. 'Absolutely. An unlimited cheque-book. Each cheque redeemable against the Ryan Wolfe Bank.'

She stroked his crisp hair, considering. 'So I get money and sex—but you'll let me have my freedom?'

'If that's what you want. If that's what it takes. And I will listen to you and learn, if you're still willing to talk to me.'

'And I get the money and the sex on my own terms?'

'Yes.' He smiled at her. 'It's a good offer. Take it.'

'I don't know,' she said. 'I need to consider.'

She needed to think.

She needed to remember.

To remember how it had been.

CHAPTER SEVEN

How it had been.

Though so many things had happened in the year since she had been with Ryan, she could remember exactly how it had been.

It was all engraved on her heart, like scenes from a story book.

Like the first time she had set eyes on him.

The old house in Hampstead was still beautiful, but in a poor state of repair. The movie was low-budget. The producers were hoping to sell it for television, their hopes bolstered by the fact that the novel the script was based on, *Ayala's Angel*, was a classic novel by Anthony Trollope, and was going to be a set text for schools and universities the following year.

The house was supposed to be the home of a fabulously wealthy mid-Victorian family. That wealth often had to be represented by extravagant flower displays, to eke out the somewhat sparse furnishings. A big chunk of the budget had gone on superb period costumes for the principal cast members, who were all very young—three of them, including the star, Annie Drummond, who played Ayala, were still drama students.

The four main actresses, in full costume, were about to do a scene in the parlour of the house. They looked delicious in flouncy Victorian dresses, seated around a gleaming silver tea-service on a low table.

A problem that had immediately been picked up was a large and obviously modern radiator, fixed to the wall immediately behind the actresses. The director, Angus Robertson, had called for Penny to work some magic, and she had been arranging a large vase of flowers in front of the offending twentieth-century appliance, while the cameras and the actresses waited.

Just as she was putting the finishing touches to the display, she'd heard the bustle of excitement and the words, 'Ryan Wolfe is here.'

She'd felt a flicker of interest at the name. Of course, even after no more than three months in the movie world, she knew who Mr Wolfe was—the legendary entrepreneur, the man who could breathe life into a movie that was failing for lack of funds. The man everyone had been hoping would come to the set of *Ayala's Angel*, love what he saw, and conjure mountains of money out of thin air.

So Penny straightened, looking over her shoulder to see the great man. She'd been expecting someone who looked like a banker, in a suit, with gold-rimmed spectacles and grey hair. Nobody had told her what Ryan Wolfe looked like.

Nobody had told her that he was the most beautiful man in the whole wide world.

Her heart seemed to jump in her breast, like a salmon leaping up a waterfall.

Ryan was standing with Angus Robertson at the edge of the set. He was wearing jeans and a denim jacket, a dark-haired man in his thirties, with a face that some pagan sculptor had carved out of bronze to break women's hearts.

His eyes were a dark grey, framed by thick black lashes,

and full of a powerful character. The brows that were set over them were also dark, their heaviness promising passion, or perhaps a fiery temper. His nose was long and straight, a Norman nose with arched and flaring nostrils.

His hair was shorter and neater in those days; he was altogether more groomed, more professional-looking than the Ryan Wolfe who was to walk into her florist's shop a year later.

But it was his mouth that made Penny go weak at the knees—the most beautiful male mouth she had ever seen, full and sensual, yet filled with authority and command. Her gaze was drawn inexorably to that mouth, and by some black magic she could feel it on her own, feel the deep, dark kiss that it seemed she had been waiting for all her life.

She saw Ryan Wolfe look her way, and felt the impact of his gaze meeting her own as an almost physical force—an earthquake shaking the floor under her feet, a strong wind rocking her body.

Movie sets were such busy places—people, cameras, lights, cables snaking across the floor, voices shouting commands of all kinds—that she had always welcomed their anonymity, the feeling that she was just a small cog in a big machine.

But that day in Hampstead she felt as though there was a klieg light poised right above her, illuminating her, making her brilliant.

She felt her skin go hot, then cold. She had trouble catching her breath. Her stomach had tied itself in a hard knot.

That was how powerful, how electric it was.

Their locked gaze only broke when Angus Robertson took Ryan by the arm and began introducing him to the actresses.

'This is Annie Drummond, who plays Ayala, Yvette Simon, who plays Lucy, Jennifer Bridges, who's doing Augusta, and Lisa Bonnie, who's playing Emmeline.'

Ryan greeted all the actresses with grave courtesy and

listened to Angus explaining a little about the scene they were going to shoot. Then he nodded, and turned to Penny, who was standing there like a statue. He said nothing, but the direction of his gaze was so intent and so apparent that Angus Robertson was compelled to fill the pause.

'And this is Penny Wellcome, our brilliant set decorator,' he said. 'She's responsible for the lovely flowers you see all around.'

Ryan took her hand in his. His grip was warm and firm. His eyes looked deep into hers. 'They are truly lovely,' he said in a quiet voice.

Penny didn't know what she murmured in reply—some platitude—but she did know that she had coloured to the roots of her hair.

The star, Annie Drummond, was a spectacular beauty. Every man in the world stared at her unashamedly, fascinated by her golden hair, cornflower eyes and perfect smile. Every man, with the exception of Ryan Wolfe. He seemed to have eyes only for Penny.

With the offending radiator covered, shooting the scene commenced. There were two cameras covering the action. The actresses were well-rehearsed and full of vivacity, so the long scene evolved without interruptions.

Ryan stood with folded arms behind one of the cameras. Penny was close by him, her heart still thudding in her breast. Why couldn't she seem to catch her breath? She felt Ryan's presence in an almost physical way—his proximity was the most sexual feeling she had experienced in months.

So that, when he turned to glance at her again over his broad shoulder, the shock of his eyes meeting hers made her feel faint, yet so alive, so aroused. She could not tear her eyes away from his. And so she read the message that was so clear in that brilliant grey gaze—that he found her as fascinating as she found him.

When the scene was over, Angus bustled over to Ryan, his eagerness apparent in every line of his face. Indeed, the whole company was intent on hearing Ryan's reaction, and there was a silent yet deafening cheer when he replied, 'I think it's utterly charming, and I'm very interested in seeing the rushes.'

It was much later, as he was leaving, that Ryan walked across the set to where Penny was helping prepare for the next scene.

'I'm having a dinner party for some friends at my flat this weekend. I think your flowers are the most beautiful I've ever seen. I want you to do the arrangements for my party. Can you help me?'

'Yes,' she said without hesitation. 'I can help you.'

That was how it began.

After that, things moved very fast. So fast, her feet barely seemed to touch the ground.

That dinner party, as it turned out, included an Oscar-winning actress and a Hollywood director who was a household name.

She made the table exquisite, preparing everything with as much style and grace as she could muster. She had always had a gift for flowers and décor, ever since she was a child. When her university career had collapsed so tragically, it had been natural for Penny to try to make a living out of that talent.

London had shown her just how highly others valued that talent. Even though working on movie sets was at best intermittent employment, Penny was so good at what she did that people who saw her work were always asking her to do parties or receptions for them.

Though she was disbelieving at first—what she did came so naturally to her that she was surprised others couldn't do it just as easily—she soon realised that what had at first seemed a stopgap could quickly become a full-time career.

Finding a part-time or full-time job would be no problem.

Florists, restaurants, agencies were all crying out for work as good as hers.

So she made Ryan Wolfe's dinner table look stunning. And then, at the last moment, Ryan invited her to stay for the meal and meet his friends.

A fairytale.

She was dazzled by the company Ryan kept—who wouldn't be? She was dazzled by the enormous apartment in Knightsbridge, by the way Ryan spoke so effortlessly about millions of dollars, famous people, big movie projects.

But that was nothing to how dazzled she was by *him*. Once you got past the sheer physical beauty of Ryan Wolfe, there was so much more—his crackling energy and sense of purpose, his formidable intelligence, his extraordinary way of looking at the world, so different from anyone she had met before.

He was a kind of magician, who put people and things together to produce wonderful new alloys. She heard someone refer to him as an alchemist, and that was how she often thought of him—a wizard who could transmute base metals into pure gold.

He made her feel very young and inexperienced. She was off-balance from the start, a sailboat caught in a hurricane, hurtling along with no control over where she was bound.

The first time she really felt how far she was getting from land was when Ryan took her to the première of *Andersen*, a film about the famous Danish children's author, which he had financed. He took her to the opening night. The première was a triumph, foreshadowing the box-office success the film was to have that summer.

They emerged from the crowded movie theatre into a perfect July evening in London, the sky still light and clear, birds singing in the trees around the square. They were on their way to the first-night party with the cast and crew. Penny felt she was in a dream, a dream that was moving very fast, almost too fast to be enjoyed.

Ryan bundled her into a cab.

'I want to tell you something,' she said as they settled into the spacious back seat.

He took her in his arms. 'You're so beautiful,' he whispered, kissing her cheeks and throat. 'I've never seen anything as beautiful as you, my precious Penny.'

Her head was swimming. 'Wait,' she begged, 'I have to tell you something important!'

'So do I,' he said, his lips warm and erotic as they hungrily caressed the delicate base of her throat. 'You are the most perfect woman I ever dreamed of.'

'Please listen to me,' she begged.

'All right. Give me your news first, then I'll give you mine.'

'I have to go back to Devon tomorrow,' she told him.

'What?' He drew back and looked at her in surprise. 'Why?'

'It's Aubrey's birthday tomorrow. He's my stepfather. I always go down to see him on his birthday.'

'You can't,' Ryan said with a smile. 'We're going to Mexico. That was *my* news.'

'I beg your pardon?'

'We're booked on a flight to Guadalajara at eleven o'clock tomorrow morning. I have to talk to some people there. I decided to give us a little holiday at the same time. First class all the way, of course.'

'But Ryan,' Penny gasped, 'I can't just go to Mexico at the drop of a hat!'

'Why not? I know you're not working this next week. And you'll love Mexico, it's a fabulous country.'

'That's not the point! Aubrey will be so hurt if I don't go and see him!'

'I'm sure your stepfather would hate the idea of you can-
celling a trip to Mexico on his account, sweet Penny.'

'Why didn't you tell me?'

'For one thing, I only decided yesterday. And for
another—' he kissed her firmly on her full lips '—I wanted
it to be a surprise.'

'But I haven't even got any clothes ready!'

'Go with an empty suitcase. I'm going to buy you a new
wardrobe when we get there.'

She felt dizzy. 'But Aubrey—'

'We'll send your stepfather a hamper from Fortnum &
Mason. I'll have one of my people drive it down personally
tomorrow, with a gift. Gold cuff-links, perhaps?'

'Aubrey's retired,' she said, dazed. 'He doesn't wear cuff-
links any longer.'

'A set of golf clubs, then?'

'Ryan, you're a crazy man! I've never bought such expensive presents for anyone in my life!'

He looked at her with a strange, wry smile. 'Haven't you
realised yet, darling? Your life has changed forever.'

And, of course, it had.

And, of course, she went to Mexico with Ryan the next
morning. She refused to let Ryan send Aubrey expensive gifts
or hampers—that gentle man would have been embarrassed
by such largesse, in any case—instead, she phoned him early
the next morning to wish him happy birthday and explain as
best she could.

He and her mother were delighted for her. After the catas-
trophe that Tom had caused in her life, they were desperately
hoping for someone stable to 'help Penny settle down'.

It didn't seem to occur to them that the kind of man who
swept her off to Mexico at a moment's notice was not exactly
going to bring stability.

Nor that a powerful, dominant male who took control of her life was exactly what Tom had been.

It was in Mexico that they became lovers.

Something else she would never forget.

The hacienda belonged to wealthy Mexican friends of Ryan's, and was set among the hills overlooking the Rio Lerma, some thirty kilometres from Guadalajara. The scenery was majestic. Penny, who had travelled little, was entranced by the rugged, arid landscape, with its mystery and grandeur.

Their hosts, the Mirandas, were overwhelmingly hospitable. There were mariachi musicians playing at their meals, tours of the Arabian stud farm, rides through the canyons and arroyos on horseback, parties and laughter.

Looking back, it was remarkable that she and Ryan had not already become lovers. They had only known one another for a matter of a couple of weeks, but in fact, though they had kissed passionately, Ryan had been what her mother would have called 'strictly the gentleman' with her.

That all changed, one starlit night, under a golden Mexican moon.

Her bedroom had a terrace that looked out over the garden. They found themselves there in the early hours of the morning, after a party where she had been introduced to tequila, drunk, as they did in Guadalajara, the home of tequila, in a cocktail with freshly squeezed orange juice. She did not know whether it was the margaritas or the moonlight that made her feel so bewitched.

Or perhaps it was just Ryan Wolfe.

Or the way he took her in his arms and kissed her. The sort of kiss she had only ever seen in silly, old romantic films. The sort of kiss Tom had never given her. The sort of kiss she had longed for ever since she was a dreamy little girl, when stars had been as bright as the ones now over her head.

He held her so tightly, kissed her so passionately. Penny felt herself melting in his arms. Her fingers wandered through the crisp curls at the back of his strong neck. She loved the smell of his hair, male and sweet.

'You're the most beautiful woman I ever saw,' he whispered, his hands caressing her back. 'The moment I saw you I wanted you so badly it made me tremble.'

'It was the same for me,' she said in a shaky voice.

The night was warm, the liquid song of birds was all around them. And then Ryan picked her up in his arms, the way she'd only seen men do in those romantic old films, and carried her to her bed, and laid her down as gently as though she were a piece of thistledown.

He undressed her slowly while he kissed her, so many times, and so ardently, that she felt her lips swell as though stung by a bee. It had never been like this with Tom, not remotely like this. Tom had never considered her feelings in the slightest, and, since he had been her only real lover in all her life, Penny had never felt her own desire grow like this— an overwhelming need that was wild and fierce and beautiful.

Ryan kissed her naked breasts, her stomach, the silky skin of her thighs. Suddenly so shy with him, she tried to stop him from kissing any further.

'What is it?' he asked.

'I've—I've never done this before,' she whispered.

He smiled, his eyes glowing in the soft darkness. 'Never?'

'Never.'

'Try it and see. It's perfectly normal.'

Not to me, she wanted to tell him. Tom had never treated her body as something beautiful—only as a thing he wanted to plunder, to loot, so that he could fill his need.

Ryan settled his broad shoulders between her thighs. He kissed her gently, his mouth telling her how wonderful he found her taste, her smell. His fingers gently spread her, so that he could unfold her petals and reach all her secret places with his tongue.

The pleasure of his kiss was the most tender thing she had ever felt. He seemed to know everything about her, so that physical delight—something that had only been fleeting with Tom—grew into a force as irresistible as that river flowing out there in the Mexican night…and she reached the place that Tom had never taken her to.

In her inexperience, she assumed that it could only happen once. She didn't know that Ryan could take her to that place again and again, as many times as she was capable of going there; that he loved to give her pleasure for her own sake, a gift freely given, no sooner given than renewed again.

His lovemaking was a universe away from Tom's. With Ryan, she felt her soul united to that of another human being. Although by then she wasn't thinking of Tom at all. She was in a world created by Penny Wellcome and Ryan Wolfe.

So much of her life had been a quicksand lately. Ryan was massive, real, the only reality she had any more.

He wanted to prolong things, savour every inch of her. But she needed him with a swelling urgency. She wanted him so badly that her whole body seemed to cry out for him. She reached for his arousal, feeling his thick hardness in her hand.

'I can't wait,' she said urgently. 'Now, Ryan.'

He mounted her, his dark face intent as he looked down at her. The moon was over his shoulder, a golden light in a velvet blue sky. Penny raised her hips to take him, whispering his name.

'Please,' she said.

'Penny,' he whispered. She was melting wet, and he pushed in, filling her completely.

'Oh, Ryan, Ryan,' she was whimpering.

'Am I hurting you?'

'No. Please, Ryan.'

He went deep into her, so deep and tender. It was a union so perfect that she felt herself start to climax already. He supported his weight on his elbows, covering her face with hot kisses. He paused, holding still so she could writhe beneath him, crushing her pleasure from him, drinking in that sweet moment.

'Don't stop, Ryan,' she commanded fiercely. 'Come to me.'

He gathered her in his arms, whispering her name, and now he gave himself to her with nothing held back. He was a powerful, big man, and he almost crushed her. She could only cling to him, transfigured by his passion. Tom had never made love to her like this. This was something beyond her experience. She felt she was floating above herself, her spirit twisting in a sinuous dance to the beat of his love.

She was crying as they climaxed together.

He kissed away her tears, telling her, 'You'll always be mine, Penny, always and forever.'

CHAPTER EIGHT

THAT was the first time. And every time after that was just as passionate and just as intense.

And everything kept moving at the same dizzying pace, like a DVD movie running on double speed.

Within a fortnight, they had travelled to Paris, Berlin and Amsterdam together, and Mexico was only a golden memory. By then *Ayala's Angel* was wrapping up. She was offered more work on a film being shot in the Hebrides, but Ryan was filling her nights and days, and she turned it down.

He gave her a credit card of her own, drawn on his bank. A gold card, naturally, with no limit.

When she went down to Devon to see her mother and Aubrey on her mother's birthday, her mother marvelled at the credit card.

'It shows how much he trusts you, darling,' she said.

Penny privately thought that it showed things were moving much too fast, but she didn't say so. 'I haven't bought a thing for myself with it,' she told her mother. 'I only use it to get things for the household.'

'I'm sure he means you to use it for yourself, darling.'

'You should go on a spending spree,' Aubrey advised with a smile. 'Buy a few little trinkets from Asprey's. That should test whether he really means it or not!'

When she got back to London after her visit, Ryan took her out to dinner at Claridge's. She had never been inside the famous Mayfair hotel, through she had passed its handsome red-brick façade many times.

The restaurant was beautiful. She had always had a weakness for Art Deco styling, and the understated elegance of the large, quiet room, with its mirrored murals and original 1920s light fittings, seemed to her to epitomise the grace of a bygone era.

'How was everybody at home?' Ryan asked her.

'Fine,' she replied. 'Very eager to meet my mystery lover!'

'We'll go down and see them soon,' he promised.

They ordered their meal. As usual when they dined out, Ryan ordered champagne and oysters to start. Penny had grown to adore champagne, though her relationship with oysters was best described as love-hate. Sometimes they seemed absolutely delicious to her, sometimes she wanted nothing more than to spit them across the room.

The oysters at Claridge's tonight were delicious, pearly scraps that melted on the tongue, leaving a haunting taste of the sea on Penny's palate.

'I want to talk to you about something, Ryan,' she said, sipping the Roederer, which was ice-cold and very dry.

'Go ahead,' he said, buttering her a slice of brown bread.

'I need your advice. You know what happened to me at university this year. Well, I have to decide what I'm going to do next.'

'Next?' he enquired.

'Well, doing flowers for the movies is great fun, but it's hardly a steady career.'

'I agree completely,' he said. He was wearing formal evening clothes. She was in a silver sheath dress that went perfectly with the décor. Even in this exclusive setting, they were a couple handsome enough to attract every eye in the room.

'So I have to decide. I'm going to be twenty-three soon. I can't just drift. I've got two ideas.'

'Yes?' he prompted.

'One is to go back to university—not the same one, of course—and finish my degree in fine arts. The other is to start a florist shop somewhere, and build up my own business.'

If she had been expecting him to look excited by her alternatives, she was disappointed. He frowned a little impatiently. 'Neither of those options appeals to me, Penny,' he said shortly.

'Why not?' she asked in surprise. 'My parents want me to finish my degree. I can see their point. But somehow, after what happened, I've lost my nerve. I'm afraid of going back to university. Is that a cowardly thing to admit to? And since I've been in London I've learned that I can make a career out of flowers and decorating. People are always asking me to—'

'I don't want you to open a shop,' he cut in. 'And I don't want you to go back to university.'

His tone was peremptory, and Penny sat back, her eyebrows raised. 'Have I said something wrong?'

'It's good that you're thinking about your future,' he said. 'I've been wanting to talk to you about it for some time, so I'm glad you raised the subject.' He was twirling his champagne glass restlessly between his strong, lean fingers. 'But why do you want to get away from me, just when we've found each other?'

'I don't want to get away from you,' she replied, taken aback.

'If you went back to university, you would be gone for whole terms at a time,' he retorted. 'And if you went to work in some shop, I would never see you at all. Of course you would be away from me!'

'Ryan, I have to sort my life out,' she said. 'I can't just drift,' she repeated.

Ryan gestured briefly at their surroundings, the tall,

gracious columns, the exquisitely dressed people, the delicate murals. 'You call this drifting?'

'Drifting in luxury,' she said with a smile, attempting to lighten the mood. 'I don't want to turn into your kept woman.'

She saw at once that she had said the wrong thing again. His eyebrows came down angrily. The waiter arrived to clear away the tray of ice and oysters, preventing him from saying anything for a moment. When the waiter had gone, he leaned forward.

'I do *not* see you as my kept woman! How can you say something like that?'

'I didn't mean to offend you. I only mean that I want to be responsible for myself.'

He was still looking grim. 'By running away from me?'

Penny sighed. 'You said you wanted to discuss things with me. So tell me, what's *your* idea about my future?' she asked.

'I want you to move in with me.'

'I need my own space.'

'You can have your own space in our apartment, darling. You won't want for anything, my love. Anything you want. Just say the word, and it will be yours.'

'That's the problem, Ryan. The more I accept from you, the more dependent on you I become. You are the most generous man I ever knew—but you're taking away my will to fight.'

'What battle, exactly, do you need to fight?' he growled.

'The battle of life,' she said with a smile. 'Ryan, I'm only twenty-two. To tell you the truth, I still don't really know who I am. I've made rather a mess of things so far! I won't ever know who I am unless I take charge of my life a little.'

The waiters had returned, and began to serve their next course. Penny watched the delicious food being set out on fine bone china with solid silver cutlery. In the silver dress, she looked lovely, very much a part of this glittering world. But inside she was feeling cold and unhappy. Ryan's face was expressionless, but she knew he was seriously displeased.

When the waiters had left them, they started to eat. But both of them were doing no more than toy with what was on their plates.

'I'm not sure if I've expressed myself well,' she said, wanting to smooth things over.

'You've expressed yourself perfectly,' he replied.

'Ryan, if I moved in with you, what would I do with myself all day?'

'You would be with me,' he replied. 'Wouldn't that be enough for you?'

'As what? Your hanger-on? Your concubine? There in your bed when you wanted me?'

'I thought you enjoyed being in my company,' he said, his eyes meeting hers.

'Travelling to four different countries in a month is something of a shock for a girl who's hardly been out of her home town before,' she said. 'But it's not so much a relationship as a whirlwind.'

'I didn't realise you didn't enjoy travelling.'

'Of course I do! I just haven't seen my flatmates for days.'

'I don't necessarily see that as a problem,' he said drily. He did not like her friends, and he made no secret of that.

'Don't sneer at them,' she said indignantly.

'I'm sorry. But most of them seem to be rootless, unemployed drifters you picked up since moving into your digs. I don't exactly find them stimulating. You know I want you to make friends among my circle.'

'Film stars and movie producers,' she said acidly.

'You've got some objection?'

'Glittery people like other glittery people, Ryan. They're not interested in me.'

'On the contrary,' he said, 'my friends all love you—you know that. What don't you like about our lifestyle?'

'Ryan, a gold card is not a lifestyle.'

He laid his knife and fork down. 'Are you deliberately trying to make me angry?' he asked in a silky voice.

'No,' she retorted, 'but I hope you're not deliberately trying to insult me, either.'

'Insult you?' he asked ominously.

'You are very generous. I've already said that. I'm grateful for the gifts, the travel, the kindness you've showered on me. But I'm not a freeloader. I don't give my love on the basis of airline tickets or designer labels.'

Ryan poured wine for them both. His face was set. He set the bottle down and leaned back. 'I want you to understand something, Penny,' he said. 'I'm not a monk. I've known many women in my life. Some have lasted longer than others. But I always knew that none of them were right for me. For my whole life, I've been looking for one woman. One special person, someone I sometimes thought I would never meet. I'd almost given up hope—until I met you. The moment I saw you, I knew you were the one. The woman I had been looking for all my life.'

Penny felt her heart constrict. She did not know whether his words were filling her with joy—or panic. 'I'm just someone you took a fancy to,' she said with an attempt at lightness.

'No,' he said flatly. 'You're the woman I love.'

'What's to love?' she asked with a shaky laugh. 'I'm just me.'

'You may not know who you are,' he said, 'but I do. And I love the person I know.'

It was the first time he had said that he loved her. The impact of his words was like a bombshell in her heart, exploding all her flimsy plans into smithereens. 'You're a very passionate man,' she said. 'I'm afraid I'm much more pragmatic.

I worry about the rent, the weather, whether I've remembered my mother's birthday.'

'Don't you know what love is?' he asked her.

'Ryan, I told you what happened to me with Tom. He said he loved me, and I thought I loved him. But it was just a trap. I lost everything I had because of it—almost my sanity, even. I'm just not ready to enter another intense relationship.'

'You already have done.'

'No—*you* have done. I'm trying to keep my head above water.'

'I can give you plenty of work, if that is what you want,' he said. 'I need to entertain a lot, and you've always made my parties wonderful successes. If you want to put that on a business footing, then we will.'

'I'll always be happy to do your parties. You know I don't want to be paid for doing that!'

'If you started a shop, then you *would* be paid for doing that—working for total strangers, instead of for me.'

'If I started a shop, I would be in control of my own life. That's what is important to me right now.'

'More important than I am to you?'

'Damn it, Ryan! Why must you turn everything into an either-or?'

'Because I don't want to lose you, just when I've found you!' he said urgently.

'Darling, you wouldn't be losing me.' She reached for his hand across the table and took it in her own. 'You would just be letting me become myself.'

'You become yourself every time I make love to you,' he said, his eyes smoky.

'That's true,' she said, 'in one sense. In another sense, the more dependent on you I become, the less myself I am.'

The head waiter, who obviously knew Ryan well, materialised at their table. 'Is everything quite all right, sir?' he asked in concern, looking at their untouched plates.

'Fine,' Ryan said impatiently, releasing Penny's fingers. 'Take it away, please.'

The plates were cleared in silence.

In the interval before their pudding—which she was sure neither of them would eat—was brought in, Penny spoke in a low voice. 'I thought you cared enough about me to want me to develop, Ryan.'

'I want you at my side,' he said with force. 'I will not let you go!'

'You may have to.'

'Don't even think about it,' he said harshly.

'Don't threaten me,' she said, her hackles rising. 'That's what Tom used to do to me.'

'I am not Tom!'

'You are becoming sufficiently like him to make me feel nauseous,' she retorted. 'Leave me and I will make sure you fail your exams. Disobey me and you will regret it. I heard enough of that for eighteen months, Ryan! I won't take any more.'

'Don't be ridiculous,' he replied, his mouth bitter. 'I am nothing like that little creep.'

'No. You're aiming for the big-creep title.'

His eyes blazed. 'You're forgetting yourself, Penny,' he said in a silky voice.

'As a matter of fact, I've just remembered who I am.' She reached into her handbag and took out the gold card he had given her, with her name engraved on it. 'I never needed this in the first place, but thanks all the same.'

She dropped the card into his wine glass, where it fell with a plop and then bobbed like a miniature, sinking, gold *Titanic*.

Then she got up, a slim figure in silver, and walked out. She passed the waiter carrying their pudding on her way to the door.

'Put it on his head,' she advised the startled man. 'It's the hardest surface in the room.'

Of course, they made it up the next day, after spending a miserable night apart.

And, of course, he forgave Penny her impertinence and she forgave Ryan his arrogance. But the damage had been done, and the subject of her independence had become a bitter wrangle between them.

Over the rest of that summer, their quarrels intensified. She was on a roller coaster, with no brakes and no control over her ups and downs.

Things had become very complicated by early autumn.

She was being drawn inexorably into the current of Ryan's life, whether she liked it or not.

Penny was learning a lot more about Ryan's work—and about the man himself. She was starting to understand that the sums of money he dealt with were astronomical by any terms. It was impossible not to be overawed by the cool way he dealt with so much money, so many personalities, such large and complex projects.

But she also felt that he was loading more and more unwelcome responsibility onto her shoulders.

She loved making his world beautiful. It was in her blood to arrange flowers and dinners and parties, and make sure everything was as graceful as she could make it.

But beneath the beautiful surface, everything had to run with military precision, and that was often her responsibility.

Catering for the very wealthy and the very famous was hardly easy. These were people used to the very best of everything. Whether it was true or not, Penny always felt that the slightest mistake would be detected at once, the smallest lapse would be glaringly obvious. It was a strain.

It wasn't just the apartment and the table and the flowers.
It was she herself who was on show each time. Ryan's partner.
The woman at his side, who chatted easily with the great and
the famous.

It never seemed to occur to him that it was not easy for her
to measure up to some of the most beautiful and fashionable
people in the world.

If she ever brought her insecurities up, Ryan would laugh
them away, telling her she was lovelier than any movie star,
more enchanting than any of them.

'You're like a midsummer rose compared to hot-house
orchids,' he told her.

'But I feel so drab, Ryan. It's so hard sometimes.'

'You're natural, my darling. Everybody adores you, can't
you see that?'

Yet Ryan also insisted that she should buy new clothes to
fit her new lifestyle. A midsummer rose she might be, but he
wanted her dressed like the hot-house orchids. Though her
personal style had always been laid-back, she found her cup-
boards filling with designer garments and accessories.

Out went her jeans and T-shirts and in came silks and cash-
meres. Her everyday jewellery went, too, replaced by expensive gifts from New Bond Street. Intoxicating as it was to be
given diamonds, Penny felt that the prettiest bracelet could
weigh like a shackle at times.

He also nudged her into changing her hair. She had worn
her deep red hair long and untidy for years. He took her to
one of the top hairdressers and it was sculpted into a shorter,
more elegant bell, which needed to be carefully blow dried
each time she washed her hair.

Nowadays, when she looked in the mirror, she saw a
woman she hardly recognised. Not Penny the student, not
Penny the laughing, light-hearted free spirit—but a poised,

assured woman, whose clothes and jewels lent her the polish of wealth, whose smiles were as carefully manufactured as though they had been designed by computer and cut into her face by laser.

She had given up the fight in one other respect, too. She no longer kept up the pretence of going back to her flat any longer. Her life was at the Knightsbridge apartment. That also meant she had lost all the friends she had made since coming to London. Which, of course, suited Ryan just fine.

He had despised them anyway.

By now, most of *his* close friends had accepted her as a fixture. She had formed warm friendships with some of them, especially with Lucinda Strong, the beautiful, middle-aged actress whose work she had always admired, and with one or two others. With some, however, she found relations a strain.

She was falling into the role that Ryan had apparently designed for her—the beautiful organiser, making sure that there were always lovely flowers, superb food, great music in Ryan's life. Entertaining his friends and spending his money. Lots of money.

The more she entered his world, the smaller she felt. She wished that it could be just the two of them together sometimes. She longed for a life with Ryan that didn't include celebrities and business partners, that wasn't demarcated by airline flights and parties and meetings. She wanted to curl up with him in bed and eat chips out of a packet and not have the phone ring or the computer chime out its message that Ryan had mail.

But that very seldom happened.

In November, they went to Milan together for four days.

Ryan had long since persuaded her to take back the disputed gold card, and she used it to buy him a leather jacket at the Armani men's boutique.

They were staying in a stylish old hotel with a view of the great square and the cathedral. The four-poster bed was an invitation to lovers, and when they came back to the room, loaded with expensive parcels, she flopped down on it with a sigh.

'Now I know what the phrase "shop till you drop" means.'

'This is a hard city to resist,' he commented. 'Want some lunch?'

'Not sure if I can manage anything after all those wonderful cream cakes we ate!'

'You disappoint me,' he grinned. 'I thought you little Devonshire girls lived on clotted cream.'

'Only if we want to turn into little Devonshire cows.' She ran her hands down her flanks. 'I've put on so much weight since we came here. Italy is purgatory for dieters.'

'You shouldn't be dieting all the time.'

'If I didn't, how would I fit into all those smart outfits you insist that I wear?' she demanded.

'In fact, you could do with fattening up,' he said, looking down at her with smoky eyes.

'Yes, you'd turn me into a roly-poly pudding if I let you. And then I wouldn't fit into any of my clothes. And then you'd get tired of me and look for a thin girl.'

'I'll never look for any kind of girl but you,' he said, kissing her.

'What, with all those starlets languishing around you?'

'Who needs starlets when I have the moon?' he smiled, slipping off her shoes.

'Oh, such a very pretty speech, Sir Ryan!'

'And such a very pretty foot, Lady Penelope,' he murmured, kissing her feet.

She wriggled as he sucked her toes. 'Don't do that; I've been walking around all morning—I'm sure my feet aren't very fragrant!'

'But I adore the way you smell and taste.'

'Nobody could adore a fat girl with sweaty feet.'

'Is that the way you think of yourself?' he asked. He kissed the soles of her feet gently. 'You're so beautiful, so delicious, don't you know it's an honour to kiss your damp little toes?'

Sexy as it was to have him kiss her feet, Penny pulled her legs away from him and hid her toes under one of the packages. 'You can have my damp little toes back when they've been in the shower!'

'Your insecurities are showing,' he sighed. 'When they've been showered, they won't be nearly so interesting.' He rose. 'I need to make a couple of calls. Check the room-service menu and order anything you feel like. I'll just have a coffee.'

He went to the next room and picked up the phone. Penny opened the windows on to the balcony, letting in the roar of the Milan traffic and the big-city smell. It was true that she was incessantly dieting these days. And always concerned about her appearance and the way she smelled.

She had never worried about those things before. She'd always thought of herself as a self-confident woman. Now she worried that her hips, always a little wider than the standard, were starting to burgeon like a Breughel peasant—or that her legs, always sturdy, were turning into tree trunks.

It was not altogether her fault. The exquisite ladies in the shops where she bought her clothes had a knack of making her feel constantly overweight. Asking for a size twelve invariably brought the raised eyebrows. *I think we only have this in a ten, madam, but I'll check.*

God forbid that she should need a fourteen.

It was so warm, almost muggy, that she pulled off her dress.

Wearing only pistachio-green underwear, she sat on the bed cross-legged, and started opening her purchases. Italian shops seemed to know how to package everything in the most graceful way; you couldn't buy a slice of tart from a cake shop without it being carefully enfolded in waxed paper and tied with a ribbon, complete with a loop for your finger.

She had taken the gold card for a romp this morning. Milan, as Ryan had said, was a hard city to be thrifty in. Mostly, she had bought presents for other people. The big expense of the morning had been Ryan's leather jacket from Armani. It was a shade of silver-grey that made his eyes even more striking.

She slipped the jacket over her own shoulders, luxuriating in its sleekness. The leather was so soft that she could squeeze it in her fingers like a handful of butter. Just the sort of sexy, sensual garment that suited him best—in her opinion, his wardrobe was much too conservative.

She rubbed the yielding lapel against her cheek, closing her eyes as she inhaled the rich smell of brand-new leather.

'Wow.'

She looked up to see Ryan leaning against the door, watching her with sultry eyes. She giggled. 'Sorry. I can't resist the feel and smell of new leather. I must have a kink.'

'There are no kinks in you,' he said softly, coming to her with the streamlined grace of a hunting animal. 'You are as smooth as cream.'

'Not high-fat cream, I hope,' she murmured, lying back as he climbed onto the bed and looked down at her.

'Double Devonshire cream,' he said, touching her throat with his tongue. 'And I'm a greedy cat who's going to lick you all up.'

'More like a Bengal tiger,' she said, running her slender fingers down his cheek. 'I thought you had important people to phone?'

'There's nobody more important than you, my darling.' He took her in his arms and started kissing her face, devouring her mouth, her cheeks, her eyelids. She arched her neck and he kissed the hollow of her throat, a favourite place he always loved to kiss. She ran her fingers through the thickness of his hair, losing herself in the scent and feel of him. 'I dreamed of you for years,' he whispered. 'And now I've found you.'

Her heart was pounding wildly. Whatever the problems between them, his physical effect on her was always like a match tossed onto hot gasoline. She pulled him onto her, her thighs parting.

She did not bother to take his new leather jacket off—and he did not bother to take her panties off, merely pulled them aside so he could enter her. They made love for a long time, looking deep into one another's eyes, taking unashamed, pagan pleasure from one another's bodies.

Each time they approach their climax together, he would deliberately hold back, slowing the tempo down—so that, when they began again, it was ever more intense, ever more profound.

At the end, Penny was crying, as she sometimes did when it had been very intense. He held her tightly, and they lay together, listening to the roar of the traffic in the piazza below their window.

CHAPTER NINE

BUT by the time they got back to London, the argument between them had flared up again, and it was as though they had never even been friends, let alone lovers.

'Why won't you move in with me?' he demanded angrily, as they drove back from Heathrow Airport. The argument had begun because she had asked him to drive her back to her digs for the night, rather than to the Knightsbridge apartment. 'What's the point of your keeping up that shabby little bedsit when you could be living comfortably at my place?'

'The point isn't comfort,' she snapped. She was tired and irritable. The flight back from Italy had been bumpy and there had been long delays at both ends.

'Would you mind telling me what the point is, then?'

'It's preserving my independence, Ryan. Without a little bit of autonomy, I can't have any self-respect.'

'That's just silly,' he retorted. 'We've just spent a heavenly few days in Milan together. Why can't we go home together?'

'Well, I need to tidy my place up,' she said. 'Water my plants. Do some dusting. And check my postbox.'

'There won't be anything to eat in your flat.'

'Oh, I'll walk down to the Chinese takeaway. I don't mind.'

'Penny, I'll wait while you do your chores. Then I'll take

you home and we'll have an early supper and a glass of wine, and go to bed together.'

'It's your home, Ryan, not mine,' she said, looking out of the window at the stream of traffic moving through the twilit streets. The London sky looked smoky, with a Victorian feel, though the haze was due to motor cars these days, not chimneys.

'It should be your home, too. Everything I have is yours, you know that by now.'

'But I haven't earned any of that. I realise I'm being selfish. I just hoped you would understand. I know you've just given me a wonderful trip to Milan, but I need to be on my own for a while.'

'Is my company so irksome?'

'Ryan, I love being with you. It's not that. I just need time to get my damp little toes back on the ground, can't you understand that? You're used to living at high speed. I'm not. You probably want to be off to Rio tomorrow. Or Moscow.'

'Neither,' he said. 'But we do have to be in Paris again next week.'

'Paris! You make my head spin!'

'I always make plenty of time for us to do movies, museums, shopping. It should not be a hardship to go to Paris.'

'It wouldn't be—if I had any choice in the matter. But I don't! I just get my orders. "Pack for Paris, we leave at 0800 hours." Sometimes I think I'd rather go down to the chip shop under my own steam than fly to Paris under yours.' She knew it was a rude thing to say, but she was angry with his domineering manner, and wanted to assert herself. She was rewarded by seeing the anger in his eyes as he glanced at her.

'Penny, you're impossible.'

'Ryan, it was just the same with Tom—'

He thumped the steering wheel of the car in frustration. 'I am not Tom! Can't you get that into your head?'

They were in a thoroughly bad mood with one another

when they reached her digs. He walked her up the stairs to her room, carrying her bag and her Milan packages.

She let herself in and switched on the light. The place looked so dreary and lonely, such a world away from Ryan's luxurious apartment, that she almost lost her resolve. She had to fight to keep her expression neutral.

'I'm sorry I shouted at you,' he said in a strained voice. 'Won't you change your mind and come home with me?'

'Thanks for everything,' she said to Ryan. 'I do appreciate it, I really do. But I'll stay.'

Ryan was looking around the joyless room, which smelled of having been shut up for too long. 'I hate leaving you in this place,' he said.

'I'm happy here,' she lied. Happiness was not what she sought here—it was peace. She opened the letter box that was fastened next to her door. A thick sheaf of envelopes fell out, each bearing the seal of a different university—the results of her enquiry letters of the week before.

Ryan watched her with narrowed eyes as she picked them all up. 'What's all that?'

'I've sent for prospectuses from some universities.' She felt and looked shamefaced. She had not mentioned the prospectuses, to avoid an argument. Now she was caught red-handed.

'Prospectuses? You're going back to university?'

'I haven't decided anything, yet,' she mumbled.

'Penny, I don't understand you,' he said grimly.

'I know you don't,' she replied. 'I'm fully aware of the fact that you don't understand me!'

'Aren't you happy with me?'

'I'm happy with *you*. I'm not happy with the lifestyle I've somehow acquired.'

'And this is your escape?' he asked, gesturing at the sheaf of letters in her hand.

'It's much more than an escape. Can't you see that?'

'Why so many?'

'I wrote to these places to find out if there are part-time courses in the subjects I want to do. That way, I can get temporary work and pay my way through. If I can do that, I can fulfil both of my goals at the same time.'

'And leave even less time for me.'

'That's a very selfish way of looking at it.'

'Penny, I'm in love with you,' he said, and his tone suggested that if he could do so, he would cure himself of that love in a heartbeat. 'How can I live without you? I work in London. What am I supposed to do if you go off to the Midlands or Scotland? See you once a month, once a term? Is it selfish to hate that thought?'

'It will only be for a while,' she said. 'When I've got my degree, I'll be back.'

'Unless you've fallen for another professor in the meantime,' he commented drily.

'Ryan, that was unworthy of you,' she snapped. 'You know I will never meet a man anything like you.'

'Then why do you want to run away from me?'

'It isn't about you, it's about me.'

'Now which of us is being selfish?' He shrugged wearily. 'OK. I won't browbeat you any longer. Enjoy your fish and chips.'

He kissed her briefly on the cheek and walked down the stairs without a backward glance. She knew he was bitterly hurt by her sending for the prospectuses without telling him. She wanted to call after him—but there was nothing she could think of to say.

She shut the door and looked around the flat.

There was suddenly such a hole in her life. The stuffy little space seemed to crowd around her with an air of dust, loneliness and melancholy. She went to the window and saw Ryan get into his car, a tall, dark figure. He drove away.

The sky was darkening, and neon was already flickering all down the street of shabby little shops.

'If you only knew it,' she whispered to Ryan's disappearing tail-lights, 'I don't deserve you, darling. And God knows you'd be better off without *me*.'

The next day was a day for reflection. She did not call Ryan, and when he called her she let the answering machine take it, and deliberately avoided listening to the message he left.

She felt a deep unease. The lowering sky and the claustrophobic atmosphere of her flatlet did not help. There were currents of anxiety stirring at the very foundations of her soul today.

She dusted and cleaned, ashamed that she had let the little nest she had once been so proud of get so neglected. When she'd done her chores she sat down and pored over the prospectuses that had come from universities all over the country—Manchester, Liverpool, East Anglia, as far afield as Wales and Scotland.

Reading the inviting descriptions of the courses and the campuses, Penny felt like a prisoner who was getting a glimpse through a barred window at a life she had once used to have.

There were photographs in the leaflets, too. Happy students attending lectures, wearing casual clothes, strolling through leafy campuses. Or wearing academic dress, holding their degree certificates.

Graduating into lives they had chosen for themselves.

She allowed herself to slip into a daydream where everything worked out just the way she wanted it—where she got her degree, opened her own florist's business, *and* kept Ryan Wolfe.

When her dreams finally turned into dust and slipped away, she went to do what she had been putting off all morning.

She checked her diary, and accepted the truth—that today she was not one month late, but two months late.

She took some money out of her purse and went out to the pharmacy to get a pregnancy-test kit.

When she called Ryan she was close to hysteria, though the dam wall hadn't yet broken.

'Are you sure?' he asked in a blank voice. He was in a meeting with a group from one of the high-street banks, and had rushed out of the conference room to take her call.

'The test kits are supposed to be very accurate,' she replied, her voice quivering with the strain. 'And I'm two months late with my period.'

'I thought you said you had everything under control?'

'I thought I did,' she replied. 'But things go wrong sometimes. You know that. I've made an appointment to do a laboratory test this afternoon. But I know I'm pregnant. I've been feeling sick every morning for a week now. And God, I've got such a headache!'

'Oh, Penny!' After the initial shock, Ryan's voice was changing. 'This is the most wonderful news!'

'What's wonderful about it?' she asked, her own voice cracking.

'We're going to have a baby!'

'Not *we*,' she snapped, '*me*. I'm the one having the baby, Ryan.'

'Penny,' he said in an excited voice, 'I have to go and cancel this meeting. I'll be with you in an hour. Please go to the apartment; I'll meet you there.'

She felt like a volcano waiting to erupt. It was the worst possible news for her. It rendered all her options null and void. All her plans, all her speculations, doubts, longings, all were cancelled out with this one stroke.

Why hadn't she run from Ryan right at the start?

She went across to Knightsbridge and let herself into Ryan's apartment. She hadn't been here since before they'd flown to Milan. The service staff had kept it spotless, but her flower arrangements were wilted and drooping.

She threw them out, feeling as she did so that she was throwing out the faded blooms of her own hopes.

Her head was aching terribly, a blinding pain behind her eyes. She grabbed a handful of headache pills from the bathroom cupboard, then stopped as she was about to swallow them. Would these affect her baby? She needed to ask someone.

She threw the pills away in disgust. Already, her every decision was being shaped by her pregnancy—she could not think of it as a baby yet. Already, she was being stopped from doing what she needed to do.

When Ryan arrived, he was alight with joy.

He swept her into his arms and held her tight. 'Oh, Penny,' he said, his mouth close to her ear, 'this is so wonderful. I know you must be feeling mixed-up about it, but that will pass. My darling, my precious one, I'm so happy.'

They sat on the leather sofa, and she looked at him with blurred eyes. 'Ryan, it's not wonderful,' she said. 'It's a disaster.'

'I want you to marry me,' he said, holding her hands.

'I don't *want* to get married,' she said, starting to cry again. 'I'm only twenty-two!'

'I love you,' he said. 'The only reason I haven't asked you to marry me up to now is because I knew it would frighten you off. But I always wanted you to be my wife, from the first moment I met you. And I want that more than ever now.'

'Ryan, I wanted to go to university. I wanted to finish my degree. I wanted to start my own business. None of that is going to happen now!'

'Not in the short term,' he agreed. 'But other things are

going to happen. Wonderful things. You're going to be so happy. Look. I got something for you.'

He gave her the blue velvet box. She opened it. Inside was an exquisite ruby necklace. The stones glowed with red fire.

'They're Burmese rubies,' he said. 'I saw this piece a few weeks ago and I knew I wanted it for you. It will set off your beautiful eyes and hair perfectly.'

'This must have cost a fortune,' she said numbly.

'Let me put it on,' he said.

Her head was pounding as he put the necklace round her throat. The headache was getting worse and worse. The red glints thrown off by the rubies seemed to pierce her eyes, making her wince.

The necklace somehow made everything much worse. It must have cost a huge amount, and it merely rammed home how much in Ryan's power she now was.

Now she didn't merely have to be the perfect girlfriend.

Now she had to present him with the perfect baby, be the perfect mother, and spend the rest of her life being the perfect wife.

Something rose up in her breast, and the tears she'd been holding back for so long filled Penny's eyes. She burst into hysterical sobs.

Ryan held her close, trying to soothe her. But her crying seemed to have no ending.

In the afternoon, she went for a laboratory test, refusing to allow Ryan to come with her. The nurse at the clinic told her that the results confirmed that she was between eight and ten weeks pregnant.

She was feeling desperate now. She went back to her own flatlet, rather than to Knightsbridge, and tried to call her mother. But she and Aubrey were away for the weekend. There was nobody she could talk to.

The nurse she had spoken to at the clinic had told her she could take painkillers in moderation, so she had taken the prescribed dose to try to combat the awful pain in her head. But it did not even budge. The headache throbbed behind her eyes, so blinding that she could not even think.

Ryan arrived, filled with concern. He sat next to her on the sofa and held a cool, damp cloth to her burning forehead.

'My poor baby,' he said. 'Let me take you to a doctor, please. You should have a check-up right away.'

'I don't want to see a doctor,' she said tightly.

'You can't stay here,' he said. 'Not any more. It's time for you to move in with me. So I can look after you. I think we should go down to Devon, too. We need to speak to your parents, tell them the good news. Tell them we're getting married.'

'We're not getting married!'

'Penny, do you love me?' he asked her.

She was silent for a long time before answering that question. The throbbing in her head seemed to have been ratcheted up in intensity by what he was saying.

'I always thought of myself as an artist,' she said at last, in a low voice. 'Not a great artist. Not even a good one. But I know I am someone who needs to create things in the world.'

'You create beautiful things,' he said.

'I have so much to learn, Ryan. I know how to arrange flowers a little. I can paint a little, draw a little. But I've just dabbled. I've never carved wood. I've never worked with stone. I've never made ceramics. I've never done mosaic—or sculpted in clay—or painted in oils. And now I never will.'

'Silly girl,' he said, smiling at the tears that spilled down her cheeks. 'You'll do all of those things. For the rest of your pregnancy you can do whatever you want. And when our baby is born, I'll get you all the help you need so you can paint or sculpt all day long.'

'You can't just start hacking a block of marble. You have to learn. You have to go to art school. That's what I'll never do!'

She was crying bitterly now, and Ryan's smile turned to an expression of concern. 'I'm going to find a doctor,' he said. 'You'd better come to the apartment right away. You can't stay in this dump any more.'

She looked at him with bleary eyes. 'Haven't you got a meeting this afternoon?'

'Yes, but I'm going to cancel it right away.'

'Don't,' she said. With an effort, Penny sat up. Her headache was worsening all the time; it had spread down her neck and into her spine now. But she made an effort to look relaxed. 'Go to your meeting. I'll pack a bag and get a taxi to Knightsbridge.'

'Are you sure?' he asked.

'Quite sure.'

She even swallowed her tears and forced a smile to her lips. It wasn't easy, but she persuaded Ryan to go to his meeting. He left her packing a bag with essential things.

But she wasn't planning to go to Knightsbridge.

She had finally seen what she needed to do. And that was get as far away from Ryan as she possibly could. It had been that final conversation that had done it—that image of herself, a prisoner in the Knightsbridge apartment, pampered and cosseted, her baby safely in the arms of a nanny, all escape cut off forever.

A midsummer rose cut off and stuck in a vase to be admired and never to feel the touch of the sun or the wind again.

Looking back later, Penny realised that her encephalitis must have been well under way even then. What she'd thought of as the worst migraine of her life must have been the early stages of the infection that would put her in a coma a few days later.

And much of the hysteria she felt was probably due to the same cause, though she didn't know it at the time. She was literally running for her life.

She packed her bag, locked the flat and took a taxi to Paddington Station. She bought a ticket to Exeter. A one-way ticket. She was not planning to come back to London any-time soon.

She found her seat on the train and settled into it, huddling into her denim jacket. It was early autumn, the train was cold, and the denim wasn't doing much of a job of keeping her warm. She had left all her fine new clothes in Knightsbridge; her clothes, the jewellery Ryan had given her, her books, her personal-care things—in fact, she had left her entire life there. The shabby little kitbag next to her held nothing but the few possessions she had brought with her to London, months ago.

As the train pulled out of Paddington, she was thinking about the new life inside her. She had a vision of a future for her and her baby. It was vague, but it was forming in her pain-racked brain.

She would register for the course that seemed to suit her best. She would go back to university. Try to find work to help her pay her way. Her mother and Aubrey would help, too; they had always offered any assistance she needed.

She would have her baby and keep going. Developing the way she wanted to develop—not according to some plan dreamed up by Ryan on her behalf.

Looking after her baby, working, making her own way.

If Ryan still wanted her, then he would have to come and find her, and take her on her own terms. She would never again be a bird in a cage, no matter if the bars were made of gold and encrusted with rubies.

But oh, her poor head hurt so much. She felt nauseous from the pain. She must be coming down with the worst flu ever. She wrapped her hands protectively across her womb, not wanting her baby to be at any risk. She knew she was building a fever. When she got to Exeter, she would go to a doctor. Her mother and stepfather wouldn't be home for a few days, so she would stay with friends until they got back. She had called Amanda John, and she would pick her up at the station.

The world flashed past the carriage window. It was a three-hour journey to the west, and she fell into a fitful doze, the pounding in her head meshing with the rush of the train's steel wheels.

The warbling of her cellphone woke her. Feeling worse than ever, she groped for the phone in her bag. A glance at the screen told her it was Ryan calling. The little red cellphone was the one link with him she had forgotten to sever.

She answered the call reluctantly.

'Hello, Ryan.'

His voice crackled with urgency. 'Penny, where are you?'

She drew a deep breath. 'I need to get away for a while, Ryan. Please try to understand.'

'Understand? Understand what?' he demanded.

'I need space. My own space.'

'Penny,' he said, obviously making an effort to stay calm, 'where are you?'

'I'm leaving London for a time. I need to work things out for myself.'

'What are you saying?' he asked urgently.

'I'm asking you to give me time.'

'How much time?' He sounded as though he could not believe what she had done to him.

'As long as I need.'

'You need to see a doctor,' he said, his voice tight. 'I've made an appointment for you to see a top gyn-ob in Harley Street tomorrow!'

'I'll go to a doctor,' she promised. 'But I don't need someone in Harley Street. I'll find someone on the NHS.'

'Penny, please come back. Wherever you are, come back to me, I beg you.'

'No, Ryan,' she said dully. 'I can't come back. It's taken all my strength to get away.'

'For God's sake, why did you need to get away from me?'

'Haven't you heard a word I've said all these months?' she asked. 'Do you still not understand?'

'Of course I've heard,' he snapped. 'And of course I understand. But we need to talk, Penny. We need to work things out. Running away won't solve anything!'

'It's the only thing I've got left,' she replied. 'We talk. But you don't listen. If you do listen, then you don't understand. And if you do understand, then you just don't care.'

'Penny—'

'Well, I can't do it any more, Ryan. I can't be a slave in satin. I'm voting with my feet.'

'Penny, please listen to me. I will do whatever you want me to. Just come back to me. I love you. That, at least, you can't deny.'

Her eyes filled with tears which spilled over and ran hotly down her cheeks. 'No,' she whispered. 'I know you love me. Nobody has ever loved me the way you do. You just don't know how to let me be free.'

'You have always been free, Penny,' he replied. 'But you never knew it.'

'If you truly loved me, you would have let me go.'

'Love is not letting go. Love is a compromise. It's neither being a slave in satin, nor running off to be three hundred miles away from me. It's something in between. A common course. Something we work out together.'

'I don't believe you want to work anything out.' She was still crying. 'You just want everything your way.'

'Penny, I'm going to find you and bring you home.'

'Listen to me,' she said, sobbing. 'If you try to come after me, I'll go to a clinic and have this pregnancy terminated.'

The words were out of her mouth before she'd even realised she had said them. They were the worst thing she could think of, to keep him at bay. She was shocked to hear herself say something so terrible.

'Penny!' he gasped.

'I mean it,' she said brokenly. 'Just leave me alone!'

She snapped the cellphone closed, switched it off so he could not call her back, and threw it into her kitbag. Then she had to run to the toilet, and was violently sick.

She cried and vomited all the rest of the journey, until the train pulled into Exeter St David's, bringing her into a red mist of pain. She blundered out onto the station, frightened by the way she felt, by the huge pain in her head.

Something was badly wrong with her, she knew that now. She needed Ryan now, with a terrifying urgency.

Amanda, her friend, was waiting for her on the platform. She greeted Penny with an exclamation of dismay.

'Sweetie, are you sick?'

'I think I'm coming down with flu, or food poisoning, or something,' Penny said. Her legs were so weak that she could hardly stand up. 'I think I'd better see a doctor.'

'We'll go to one straight away,' Amanda said, taking Penny's bag. 'You look awful, love.'

'Wait.'

Penny dug in her bag and unearthed the cellphone. She switched it on and called Ryan's number in London. She didn't even get a ringing tone. The voice-mail service cut straight in, requesting that she leave a message.

She stood there on St David's Station, with the little phone to her ear, wondering what message she could possibly leave him. An apology for what she had done? A plea that he come and rescue her from her foolishness?

'Come on, sweetie,' Amanda said, worried by Penny's dazed condition. 'Let's get you to a doctor.'

Penny shut the phone without another word and switched it off.

She never switched it on again.

CHAPTER TEN

'WHAT happened to the van?' Ariadne squealed.

Memories of the past dissolved around Ariadne's yelp of dismay, very much of the here and now. She looked at her friend. 'I went through a hedge backwards,' Penny said.

'Oh, Penny! Were you hurt?'

'Not a scratch,' she replied, taking a huge bunch of sweet peas out of the back of the van.

'But the poor van is all scraped and dented. The paintwork will need to be redone,' Ariadne said. 'It'll cost a bomb. And what on earth are you going to do with all those sweet peas?'

'Our new client will be paying for the bodywork,' Penny said. 'And also for the sweet peas.' She smiled brightly. 'Do you know how much sweet peas in winter cost?'

Ariadne was halfway through taking off her coat. She froze in astonishment. 'Which new client?'

'Ryan Wolfe of Northcote Hall, dear. The accident happened while I was driving through the snow on business for him, so I think it's fair he should pay. Don't you?'

'Ryan Wolfe? Are you serious? You changed your mind?'

'We're going to be doing flowers and décor for his parties from now on,' Penny said. 'I'm also going to be decorating his house.'

'What?' Ariadne gaped.

'From top to bottom.' Penny laid the fragrant bundles of sweet peas on the work bench. 'And a little intimate dinner party for six tonight. They'll be swimming in sweet peas. Very, very expensive sweet peas.'

Ariadne's green eyes were sparkling. 'Penny, stop for a moment. How did all this happen? On Wednesday you said you would have nothing to do with the man!'

'Let's just say he made me an offer I couldn't refuse,' Penny said, beginning to sort the sweet peas into bunches.

'Let's just say he took you to bed and you suddenly saw the light,' Ariadne said, meaningfully. 'You lucky little devil! No wonder you're looking so smug. God, I'm green with envy! I think I'll put poison in your coffee.'

'It wasn't like that.'

'Oh? What was it like, then?'

'I don't want to go into details,' Penny said.

'Darling, the details would no doubt scorch these delicate ears of mine.' Ariadne's dark face was alight with a mixture of amusement and jealousy. 'But please don't spare me on any account. To those of us who don't currently have a sex life, due to not finding any male who is not a total pig, a little salacious detail is meat and drink. Tell me what that beautiful brute did to you! What you did to him! Give me the whole picture or I'll die of mortification!'

Penny paused in her work, her violet eyes thoughtful. 'He gave me control,' she said simply.

Ariadne clapped her hand to her mouth, her sparkling eyes wide. 'No! You tied him to the bed!'

'Oh, Ariadne, I don't mean it in that sense,' Penny sighed. 'I mean, he gave me control of my feelings. He's offered me an arrangement that lets me have space. He's willing to let me have things on my own terms. And,' she added meaningfully,

'I mean to have them on my own terms! If he is foolish enough to let me call the tune, then call it I will. And let him see how he likes it.'

Ariadne frowned. 'That's the deal?'

'He says he is willing to listen to me and try to figure me out,' Penny said with a smile.

'Really?' Ariadne said. 'Both my husbands left in the early listening-and-figuring-out stages.'

'Oh, he doesn't really mean it,' Penny said. 'He'll pretend to hear every word I say, but he'll go his own sweet way, as he always does.'

Ariadne's eyes were suddenly serious. 'Watch out for your heart, Penny.'

'What do you mean?'

'I mean that you're probably deeper in love with him than you'll ever know. You ran from him once before and he came to find you. If you push him away again, he might think you're serious. Lose this one, and you'll spend the rest of your life regretting it, I promise you that!'

Penny stared at Ariadne in surprise. Then the back door opened, interrupting them.

'Good morning, earth people.' Miles Clampett came into the workshop, grinning, as pleased as ever with himself. 'How are my two favourite humanoids?'

'Butt out, Miles,' Ariadne said vigorously. 'I was talking to Penny.'

'Well, talk about this,' he suggested, holding out an envelope. 'My fee for fixing the door. I think you'll be able to tell by the thickness of the envelope that I have charged handsomely for my extraterrestrial powers.'

'You can take it away and add fifty per cent,' Penny said.

'What?' Miles blinked. 'Add fifty per cent? You mean cut fifty per cent.'

'You heard me, Great Khan of the galaxy Rip-Off. Add a few more bags of nails and a new electric saw.'

He gawped. 'Surely you jest. You haven't even read the total.'

'Don't need to. My principal will be paying it. He can read it.'

Miles scratched his sawdust-covered head. 'It's no fun overcharging clients unless they struggle and fight.'

'Sorry to disappoint,' Penny said serenely, trimming the bunches of sweet peas.

'But it shall be as you say. Earthlings are very strange,' Miles concluded as he left. They heard him drive off.

Ariadne shook her head. 'He's right. You're acting very strangely. Are you really going to charge Miles's bill to Ryan?'

'Oh, yes.' Penny was humming to herself. She had awoken this morning with the decision already taken. She would accept Ryan's offer. After all, it was not often one got to turn the tables in life.

Ryan had given her no choices while she'd been living with him in London. Now she was going to enjoy confronting him with the same take-it-or-leave-it lack of alternatives.

He'd invited her to use him. Well, she would. On her own terms.

And she might as well take his money, too. Sex and money were two things Ryan was very good at.

If he insisted that he could not survive without her skills—when London was full of decorators and florists—then let him pay for the privilege.

She would have Ryan on her own terms.

And as for Ariadne's warning—that she was deeper in love with Ryan than she would ever know, and that if she lost him she would regret it for the rest of her life—well, those things only happened to women who were not in control. She was in control now, and she would not lose that control for anything in the wide world!

'The table's going to be beautiful tonight,' she said, tilting her head on one side to examine the flowers. 'Chains of sweet peas going from each place setting to the next. A huge spray of arum lilies in the middle. Wreaths of ivy and posies of red and black hellebores. A nice autumnal touch, don't you think?'

'It sounds wonderful,' Ariadne said.

'I've ordered four silver candelabra from Legacy, the wedding place—huge ones, a dozen candles in each. And I ordered crystal and porcelain tableware from them, too. They've promised to get it all to Northcote by four this afternoon. And the prettiest damask table linen you ever saw.'

'You rented all that for one party?'

'Bought, darling, bought.'

'Penny!' Ariadne gasped. 'It's going to cost him a fortune.'

'Your point being…?'

'He'll quickly get sick of this level of expenditure!'

'Then he can go back to London,' Penny said calmly, 'and stop pretending things he doesn't mean.'

'Oh, Penny,' Ariadne said, 'don't kill the goose that laid the golden eggs. And don't chase him away—he's too beautiful!'

'He asked for it,' was her reply. 'He'll get it.'

'What about food? Are we going into catering, too?'

'No. He says he has that covered.'

'But the kitchen hasn't even been set up at Northcote, has it? And he has no staff.'

'No.' Penny shrugged. 'It's his business. I'm just taking care of the presentation. For all I care, he can open a tin of beans. Beans and sweet peas,' she hummed. 'Very tasteful.'

Ariadne giggled. 'You're terrible. And who is coming to this impromptu bash with the silver candelabra and the baked beans?'

'Some movie people. And Cameron Ray and Lenka Manchester.'

'You're joking,' Ariadne gasped. 'Cameron Ray!'

'It's their third wedding anniversary. You know how dogs live seven years to each human year? It's the same with Hollywood marriages. So this is actually their twenty-first wedding anniversary. A big occasion.'

'Sneak me into the house,' Ariadne begged. 'I just want to breathe the same air as Cameron Ray!'

'You can help me set things up this afternoon,' Penny promised, 'and maybe you'll get a glimpse of His Cameronship—though I warn you, you may be disappointed. Now, let's get to work!'

Ariadne was not only breathing the same air as Cameron Ray by nine o'clock that evening, but she was also blissfully inhaling his cigar-smoke.

The young Californian heartthrob, with his thatch of tow-coloured hair artfully disarranged as always, was puffing contentedly at a cheroot between courses. His lovely wife, Lenka, was in animated discussion with Ryan.

Penny had to admit that everything looked wonderful. She and Ariadne had worked hard. The table was glorious.

The formal dining room, though bare of anything except the table and chairs, was such a stately setting, with its magnificent moulded ceilings and imposing Adam fireplace. The four huge silver candelabra glowed warmly, illuminating the laughing faces of the guests. A fire burned brightly in the hearth. Apart from that, the room was empty, and dancing shadows took the place of the rich furnishings that would one day be arranged here.

The house seemed to be coming to life in some strange way, even before she began her work. Ryan was working his magic with it, too.

She had agreed to stay for the guests' arrival so that Ariadne could see the Rays. But as they had all arrived in their taxis and limos there had been a chorus of greetings for her from each one, and with the warm embraces and kisses her heart had lifted. Though she'd planned to be out of the house as soon as her work was done, she had ended up staying for dinner, and the enchanted Ariadne had been invited, too.

She took in the faces around the table now. There were two well-known British actors, one with her handsome new American husband, the other with his male partner of many years, an Italian producer couple who had been involved in some of Ryan's projects, and finally the Rays, genuine Hollywood royalty.

'Have you been on a world cruise, Pen?' Cameron grinned. Ryan had seated Penny, somewhat to her dismay, at the head of the table, as though she were the hostess. 'Or locked away in some convent?'

'I've been on sabbatical, working,' she said awkwardly.

'Seems to have done you good,' he told her, giving her the benefit of his bedroom eyes. 'You look sweet enough to eat.' His wild ways were legendary, but privately Penny thought that his sex-appeal was nothing compared to Ryan's.

Flavia Pollini, one of the Italian producers, leaned forward. 'This table setting is exquisite, Penny,' she said. 'It's like a fairy princess's wedding.'

'You do things so beautifully,' her husband agreed. 'It is so good to see you and Ryan together again.'

She smiled and murmured some innocuous reply. How many times was she going to have to field that remark?

And how was Ryan planning to feed all these people in such a bare—though imposing—house?

Resourceful as ever, Ryan had compensated for his lack of staff by hiring in one of the mobile catering companies who provided food for crews and actors on location. No beans for him.

Though Ryan had placed her in the position of hostess, there was nothing she needed to do but join in the fun.

The menu was Cantonese. A supply of scrumptious Chinese dishes in cartons flowed from the kitchen and everybody dipped in with abandon, with the happy high spirits Penny remembered from so many film sets.

Apart from Cameron Ray's crack about the convent, as though by common consent, nobody was tactless enough to ask Penny where she had been for the past year.

'It's good to have you back,' Roland Quincy murmured, patting her hand. 'I miss your gentleness.' On screen, he was one of the funniest men in the movies, but his off-screen presence was more introspective. Penny knew that he suffered from depression, and she was always especially sensitive with him, something he appreciated in a world where he was expected to always be the clown.

Welcomed among them all, with a glass of champagne in her hand, Penny realised how much she had missed occasions like this one. It was amusing to watch Ariadne, who was positively starry-eyed, drinking it all in. She recalled herself when Ryan had first brought her into this world, how new it had all seemed.

Familiar though she was with it, it was still wonderfully stimulating to be among creative people again, people who achieved big things. She listened carefully, trying to pick up what they had all been doing since she had fled the London scene a year earlier.

The talk, indeed, was animated movie talk. Ryan, she quickly realised, was lining Cameron Ray up to play the lead opposite Lucinda Strong's Tamara in *The Other Side*. Cameron had played a string of action comedies lately, and was interested in doing something more serious. But he was initially derisive of this role.

Ryan was explaining the concept to Lenka, who was looking enthusiastic at the prospect of Cameron playing opposite a leading lady who, for once, was not the sex goddess of the moment. Involving Lenka was a shrewd move—she was one of the few people who had any influence over her wayward but box-office-pleasing husband.

'The film starts out in New York,' Ryan was saying, 'after the war. The costumes and sets are so elegant. Tamara is a very wealthy, very lonely woman in her fifties, and Christopher is a penniless young ex-serviceman. She leads him on a journey of sexual and emotional discovery. They travel to Europe on a grand tour. They revisit his battlefields and she heals his emotional wounds. It's a very erotic, but very poignant story.'

'It sounds perfect for Cameron,' Lenka said, running Penny's sweet-pea chains through her fingers.

'And if old Lucinda looks too gruesome in a lacy nightie,' Cameron grinned, 'we can always slap a pot of Vaseline on the lens, can't we, Ryan?'

Cameron was the only one who laughed at his own humour. Penny could not help wincing at the slighting reference to Lucinda. Cameron Ray was a rough diamond, to put it charitably, but Penny knew that, when the film was cut into its final version, his performance would project only the charismatic sensitivity that his public loved so much. Such was the magic of the movies.

Flavia Pollini touched Penny's arm, drawing her attention away from the young star. 'This house is so beautiful. I adore it. But I'm surprised Ryan is planning to buy it—and moving out of London. I'm sure all of this is your idea.'

'Oh, no,' Penny replied, taken aback by the suggestion.

'It's his idea, I assure you. He says he's tired of the Knightsbridge flat.'

'Perhaps I put that badly,' Flavia smiled. 'I should have said, this is your influence.'

'I have no influence with Ryan Wolfe,' Penny laughed.

Flavia shook her glossy head. 'We both know that's not true. And this house is clearly conceived as a perfect showcase for you. A garden for an English rose to bloom in.'

'No, Flavia, you're wrong.'

'Ryan was telling me earlier that he has handed over all the decorating and furnishing to you?'

'Yes, but—'

'He wants you to fit into this house perfectly.' Flavia's brown eyes were wise. 'You, and the children you will bring him.'

Cameron made some fresh joke. Among the laughter, the pretty girls from the catering company brought in freshly steaming cartons. Cameron Ray turned his handsome face to Penny, his lips curling around the cheroot clenched between his whiter-than-white teeth.

'Penny, can you really see me romping between the sheets with a woman old enough to be my mother?' he scoffed.

Penny, her mind still whirring around the things Flavia had been saying to her, retorted without thinking. 'You should be grateful to even be considered to play opposite an actress of Lucinda's calibre.'

She saw Cameron's eyes widen in surprise, and there was a sudden silence round the table.

Coming to her senses, she did her best to repair any damage she might have done. 'Lucinda's experience will make a perfect foil for your huge talent, Cameron,' she said earnestly. 'Playing opposite Hollywood beauties, you always have to share the limelight. But Lucinda is such a wonderful supporting actress—she knows how to make the star look good.

You'll be the only one on the screen. I think you'd be unforgettable in the role.'

Cameron's frown eased. 'You think so?'

'Absolutely,' she assured him. 'And if you don't take the part, one of your rivals will jump at it—and you won't be the one walking up on stage to claim your Oscar next year!'

There was more laughter. Cameron turned to Ryan, looking thoughtful, and started asking questions in a serious undertone.

Ryan dropped her an almost imperceptible wink over Cameron Ray's shoulder. Suddenly, Penny had such a powerful sense of *déjà vu* that she had to catch her breath. Ryan had manoeuvred her so cleverly tonight! She had fallen into his trap without even noticing!

She had slipped, without even thinking, into the role he had planned for her. Playing gracious hostess to his party, using her beauty and charm to achieve his aims, working in harmony with him to give his friends a happy time, and yet also achieve his goals.

Damn him! How was it that he always managed to get his own way?

The party did not start to break up until well past midnight. Snow had started to fall again, and it was that, more than anything, that made guests start thinking about the road home.

In the general confusion of guests finding coats and bags, exchanging kisses and farewells, Ariadne hurried up to Penny.

'You'll never guess,' she said with sparkling eyes. 'The Rays have offered me a lift home in their limo!'

'Nice,' Penny said. Ariadne always managed to organise things.

'I'm going to ask them to drop me off outside the pub,' she giggled. 'Can you imagine everyone's faces? Me, being dropped off from a limo, after an evening with Cameron Ray and Lenka Manchester!'

'I love it.'

'And they're such an adorable couple!' Ariadne hissed, dashing off. 'I wish I'd known you mixed with such famous people!'

Penny smiled as she watched her friend leaving with the movie stars. Cameron, for all his good looks, was a selfish and vain philanderer; Lenka, desperately hoping for a baby to keep her wandering husband at home, was growing increasingly neurotic; but Ariadne saw none of that. She saw only their star quality. Mixing with 'such famous people' was just like mixing with un-famous people—there was good and bad in all of them.

She started pulling on her own coat, ready to leave. Ryan walked up to her, smiling. 'Have a nightcap with me.'

He was wearing jeans and a dark blue shirt. The colour suited him, making him look warm and sexy. She considered his offer. 'OK,' she agreed, hanging her coat back up again, 'but just one.'

'Good.' He poured them both a whisky on the rocks, and then stretched out his hand to her. 'Come. I want to show you something.'

Penny took his hand, feeling his warm fingers twine possessively around her. He led her upstairs.

'Your table setting was the prettiest thing I've ever seen, Penny, magical and lovely.'

'There was a Christmas dinner in this house in 1899. It was very special, because the new century was going to begin in a few days. The flowers that night were the same—chains of sweet peas, wreaths of ivy, a display of arum lilies and hellebores.'

'Now, how on earth do you know that?'

'I've been doing some research into Northcote. The

owners have sold so many of the treasures that used to be here. I want to know what it was like in its glory days, so I can restore it properly.'

'Are there records?'

'Of course. If you look hard enough. Local newspaper archives are especially useful. This house was always in the news, and there are lots of descriptions of parties and receptions. Lots of photos, too. Then there are books on art history with references.'

'You amaze me,' he said. 'And I love the things you've bought. The crystal, the dinner service, the candelabra, they're all absolutely perfect.'

'I'm happy that you're happy. It was a fun evening,' she said.

'And you handled that little squirt perfectly,' Ryan smiled. 'If he wasn't the best-looking man in Hollywood, I wouldn't consider inflicting him on Lucinda. But the truth is, they will go perfectly together in the final cut.'

'I agree.'

Ryan led her to the window of his bedroom. They looked out.

Snow was drifting down steadily and silently. But there was a gap in the clouds, and through it a full moon was shining down with silvery brilliance.

Snow had carpeted the lawns, blurring the contours of the land. The huge trees, many of them planted by Capability Brown in the early eighteenth century, and now two centuries old, wore veils of white. The sweep of parkland had an unearthly beauty. The landscape appeared to glow in the strange light.

'Isn't it ravishing?' he murmured, holding her close.

'You'll tire of it,' she predicted. 'You can't pop round the corner to Harrods' Food Halls for caviare and crackers.'

'I've stopped lunching off caviare and crackers,' Ryan said. He was holding her close in his arms. 'More importantly, children can't play in the Brompton Road. Here they can run free.'

'Children?' she repeated uneasily, remembering what Flavia Pollini had said to her a few hours earlier.

'This is a grand mansion, as you once said. But much more than that, it's a family house. The moment I saw it, I knew this would be a wonderful place to bring up children. To make a home.'

She pulled out of his arms uneasily. 'You don't want children. You don't want any ties.'

'Perhaps it's too soon for you to understand,' he said gently. He looked into her eyes. 'Do you want to stay the night?'

They were standing by the four-poster bed. Its cream feather quilt was laid open invitingly. 'No, thank you,' she said quickly. 'I'm going to go home.'

He did not argue, merely smiled faintly and nodded. 'Whatever you want.'

She drained her glass and handed it to him. 'Thanks for the nightcap. And I'm glad you liked my work and the things I've bought. Goodnight, Ryan.'

She kissed him briefly on the cheek, catching a hint of his cologne.

'Please drive carefully this time,' he said.

'I will, I promise. And they've cleared the roads today. You don't need to follow me.'

And then she was hurrying down the stairs.

Penny emerged from the warmth of the house into the cold, yet somehow soft air of a snowy night. An owl hooted in the trees.

She walked to her van. She glanced over her shoulder as she opened the door. The windows of the great house glowed like jewels.

It was a strange feeling to be leaving. A very strange feeling.

She was doing something she had never done in her life before—walking away from Ryan.

Not running. Walking away.

And he was not chasing after her.

She opened the door and got into the van. She had done it. She had made a dignified exit. Said goodnight. Kissed his cheek. Left.

She was in control.

It was as easy as that.

Now all she had to do was drive through the cold, dark night, get to her cold, dark cottage, and get into her cold, dark bed. Alone.

Penny watched the snowflakes drifting down onto her windscreen for a while, feeling the hollow place open up inside her.

Then she got out of the van, locked the door, and walked back into the house.

He was standing where she had left him, beside the bed. His beautiful grey eyes met hers with warmth, but no mockery.

'I changed my mind,' she said simply.

'It's your choice,' he replied in a quiet voice.

'Are you glad I did?' she asked, slightly hesitant.

For answer, he held his arms out to her. She went to him, and he drew her close against his muscular body. He kissed her mouth, and she felt herself melt in his arms.

It was a long, sweet kiss, filled with yearning and tenderness. Her heart was pounding in her temples. Goose-bumps washed along her arms and tightened her nipples.

Ryan laid her down on her back on the bed, and reached under her skirt to slide her panties off. He kneeled at the side of the bed while she lay back.

'I need you so much,' he whispered.

Ryan slipped her slim thighs onto his shoulders and leaned forward to kiss the pink orchid of her sex. His mouth was so warm and so sensitive. The pleasure he gave her was so intense, and yet so tender.

He knew her responses as well as though he had looked into her secret mind. He knew how to be patient when she needed more time, he knew how to prolong her delight to the utmost, and then start all over again before she even knew she was ready.

When the ache to have him inside her grew too much, she called to him, and he came to her. The weight of his body, the way his desire thrust deep inside her, these were things that drove away fear and doubt, as though when he made love to her there was no room for the panic that so often rose in her when she was with him.

They climaxed together, as they always did, and then lay still, their bodies ravelled together like driftwood smoothed and tangled by the sea. The moon shone brilliantly in at their window.

'Now,' he whispered to her, 'is a perfect time for me to do some learning. So talk to me, Penny. Tell me all about you.'

CHAPTER ELEVEN

IT WAS not exactly a great insurrection, she thought wryly. She had only got as far as her car before turning back and going to Ryan's arms.

But the important thing was that it had been *her* decision. Her decision to leave, which he had not disputed. Her decision to go back to him, which he had welcomed. That made a big difference. For the first time, silly as it seemed, Penny felt that she was not being driven along by the force of Ryan Wolfe's personality. There was space for her and her decisions.

It had also made a difference that Ryan had asked her to talk about herself, and had listened while she spoke. It had not been long before she'd drifted off into sleep, of course. She'd been too tired for any great heart-to-heart revelations. But it had been a start.

Over the weeks that followed, Penny's time was increasingly taken up with Northcote Hall. The job was far bigger than she had dreamed of when she'd decided to accept Ryan's invitation. Northcote had eight bedrooms, ten bathrooms, four reception rooms, a library, a huge kitchen, a music room, a games room—not to mention half a dozen utility rooms of various kinds, and a large guest cottage.

'I made the owners an offer yesterday,' Ryan told her.

She had opened her eyes at that. 'You did?'

'Yes—a good one, too. Just a little less than they are asking. I don't believe in trying to haggle for something I really want.'

'Then they should accept,' Penny had said, looking up into his magnificent face.

'If they have any sense, they will,' he'd agreed.

'Ryan, this is a huge step for you,' she had said seriously. 'It's very different from a few paintings or a new kitchen. I know you're a rich man, but if you change your mind you might not be able to sell a house this size for a long time. You'd have a lot of money tied up.'

'I've made my mind up,' he'd replied simply.

Decorating this house was going to be a long-term job. Early on, she took the decision to start with the essential rooms, and get them finished before considering the rest of the huge house. From the point of view of Ryan's work, that meant the kitchen, the dining room and the reception rooms. He could continue camping in the master bedroom and living out of a suitcase until the rest of the house was finished.

True to his word, Ryan gave her a cheque-book and a credit card to make purchases for the house. Using his credit card brought back some strange memories.

She used his money to good effect, ordering a custom kitchen from one of the most reputable firms, comfortable furniture for the reception room, and a selection of handsome antique pieces.

She hoped that Ryan had meant it when he'd told her the budget was large; the bill was already mounting steeply—she was buying the very best of everything.

But she knew what Ryan wanted to do with Northcote. He was planning it as the centrepiece of his business, a beautiful place where his friends and business associates could meet in relaxed, luxurious surroundings to discuss projects, away from the bustle of the capital.

Northcote soon filled with workmen, some commissioned by Penny, others by Ryan himself. The stables were being refurbished, and soon there would be horses available for guests to ride through the beautiful parkland.

One of the reception rooms was already being set up as a private movie theatre with plush seats and the most hi-tech equipment available.

A seminar room was being installed in the office, with international video-conferencing facilities.

Through it all, Ryan kept on working. *The Other Side* was now taking shape. Having secured his two stars, Ryan now had real interest from the independent studios. They were bidding against each other to produce this film.

The potential of the film was becoming clear—it would be the sort of lush, sexy, poignant production that garnered both critical acclaim and box-office success. Visitors kept coming to Northcote, and Penny had to arrange three big dinner parties in two weeks.

She and Ryan were together every day—and almost every night.

He was true to his word. He had changed in a subtle but definite way. Though she consulted him about all the major decisions, he had meant it when he'd told her she would be mistress of Northcote; she was free to shape the house as she saw fit.

Though his lovemaking was still the overwhelming storm of pleasure and passion it had always been, she no longer felt that she was being carried along like a helpless passenger on a locomotive.

After the dinner party one Sunday night, they went up to Ryan's bedroom with a nightcap of a whisky on the rocks. It had become their custom to do this. Ryan, who had been wearing a dark grey Armani blazer, took it off and draped it over the back of a chair.

'When are you going to start working your magic on our bedroom?' he asked, smiling at her. 'It's still as bare as ever it was.'

'For one thing, it's not *our* bedroom, it's *your* bedroom,' she replied tartly. 'And for another, I'm keeping my priorities straight. You can keep pigging it here, out of sight, but you need to be able to entertain your glittery friends!'

He slipped an arm round her waist and kissed her mouth. 'Whatever you say,' he said, his breath warm against her neck. 'You're the boss.'

'And don't you forget it,' she said, closing her eyes as his kisses trailed round the sensitive skin of her throat to the delicate line of her jaw.

'Don't worry, I won't. I know my place.' His mouth brushed hers, a delicious kiss like the touch of an angel's wing. 'I saw those oil paintings you hung in the corridor. They're beautiful.'

'They should be. You paid a fortune for them.'

He laughed softly. 'They'll be here forever. Like me.'

'You're really staying forever?'

'Definitely. The place is growing on me.' He kissed her mouth in the same way as before, except this time the angel's wing hovered a little longer on her susceptible lips.

Then he kissed her eyelids, one after another, making her shiver with sensual hunger. 'I want you, Penny. Can I have you?'

'Maybe,' she replied. 'Talk me into it.'

'As if you were a studio chief?'

'A studio chieftainess,' she replied.

'I'll do my best,' he said, with a glint in his eyes. 'Well, Miss Watkins—or may I call you Penny?'

'I think "Miss Watkins" will do for the time being,' she said coolly.

'Miss Watkins, I have a project in mind.' His fingers were caressing the curves of her breasts through the silk shirt she wore—and somehow, her buttons were being deftly unfastened. 'A project that really excites me so much.'

'We're already committed to several new projects, Mr Wolfe,' she replied. 'I doubt whether we can consider anything new this year. Perhaps in a couple of years' time.'

'Oh, Miss Watkins, I would hate to think of you missing the boat.' His mouth brushed hers delicately. 'This is truly something special. I chose Watkins Productions because you're so wonderful with thrusting new ideas like this one.'

'What's it all about?' she asked, tilting her head back as he opened her shirt and kissed her throat.

'It's a love story,' he said quietly, kissing the curve of her breasts, while his fingers unfastened the belt of her trousers. 'About two people who are absolutely, insanely in love with one another.'

'Sounds like old hat to me, Mr Wolfe.'

'It's the oldest hat there is,' he agreed. 'As old as Adam and Eve. And just as successful.'

'Have you got a good script?'

'The script is wonderful, Miss Watkins. The sweetest story you ever heard. There's just one thing. It's not finished yet. It's still being written.'

'And when will it be finished?'

'Maybe never,' he said. He unzipped her trousers and slid them down over her hips. 'Mmm, Miss Watkins, may I compliment you on this underwear? It's very, very pretty. What colour is that?'

'The box said, "Wild Cherry,"' she said, feeling goose-bumps wash over her skin as he caressed her.

'It makes your skin look like cream,' he whispered. She was wearing only the deep pink underwear now. He stripped off his own clothes, his splendidly muscled body rippling in the firelight.

Then he came to her. His skin was hot against hers and she could feel his strength just below the velvety surface.

'You were talking about the project, Mr Wolfe, not my underclothes!'

'The project and your underclothes are intimately linked, Miss Watkins,' he said with a smoky smile. 'You might say the one cloaks the other. And I think I can guarantee that this will be very fulfilling.'

'Indeed?'

'Oh, yes. It will be the best decision you ever took. I promise you'll be pleased with the final result, very pleased indeed.'

'How can I be pleased when the project will apparently never be finished?' she demanded.

'You'll never want it to finish.' Ryan reached around her back to unfasten her bra. Her nipples brushed his chest as he kissed her mouth, not like an angel's wing this time, but like a lover claiming his mate. 'That's what's so special about this one,' he whispered hotly in her ear. 'Other projects all come to an end. Not this one. This one will last forever.'

He had slipped his thumbs into the waistband of her panties, and now he pulled them down so that they slipped down to her ankles. She stepped out of them. 'Is this part of your usual approach, Mr Wolfe?'

'I believe in getting to grips with my subject, Miss Watkins.'

Penny snorted. There was deceptive strength in her slim body, and she used it to push him onto the bed on his back. Pressing her palms on his broad, muscled chest, she slid her thigh over his and straddled him. Amusement and desire were swirling into a dangerous cocktail in her heart. She wanted him, yet she wanted to dominate him, the way he had dominated her. 'You're a persuasive man, Mr Wolfe!'

'That makes two of us, then.'

Penny stroked the rippling muscles of his stomach. 'You've lost so much weight. You used to be sleek, like a well-fed lion. Now every muscle and sinew is showing.'

'Don't I please you any longer?' he demanded.

'You will always be the most beautiful man I've ever seen,' she said simply. 'And the most impossible.'

'Untie your hair,' he pleaded. 'Let me see it.'

She had pulled her dark red hair back into a pony-tail. Now she reached up to unloose the ribbon. His eyes followed the way her breasts lifted with the movement. She unfastened the band and shook her pretty head. Her silky hair fell around her smooth face in two dark waves. As if in a dream, he reached up and stroked the silken tresses.

Penny leaned forward and kissed his parted lips. She felt her soft breasts swing against his muscular chest.

Ryan's manhood was swollen and hard against her body His strong hands cupped her slim waist and guided her hips over him so that he was poised to enter her.

'I need an early answer, Miss Watkins,' he said, the tension audible in his voice. 'I can't keep waiting for much longer.'

'Why? Will you lose interest?'

'No. I may just have to push ahead on my own.'

'You're known for being a very pushy man. But I advise you not to try that approach with Watkins Productions. Make sure you have my personal approval before going ahead!'

'Please, Miss Watkins,' he said softly.

Penny heard her own whimper of desire as he pressed his erect body against the swollen sensitivity of her own. All she had to do was move slightly, and he would be able to enter her. But he waited. He was leaving it up to her, that all-important decision.

Penny took it without thinking.

She heard him call her name as she sank down slowly on him. He pierced her deep inside, a fulfilment that was at once shockingly intense and profoundly familiar. She was panting, her eyes half-closed as she watched his face. 'How does that feel, Mr Wolfe?' she whispered, her voice thick with desire as she pressed down on him with her hips.

'Penny, I need you so much.'

She cried out, longing and desire mingled in an inarticulate sob. He rocked her against him, so that with each movement her most sensitive zones thrust against his solidity.

At first she was fiercely demanding, digging her fingertips into his shoulders, her hips thrusting into him. Then, as she knew that they were both rushing towards an inevitable climax, her movements gentled, became slower and more languorous, surer of purpose.

She watched his face intently, wanting to release at the precise moment he did. And then they were there. He called her name a dozen times as he surged within her, heat exploding deep between them.

When their shuddering ceased, Penny's head was drooping like a lily on a broken stem. She sank into his arms and he held her close, his mouth buried in her fragrant hair. The moonlight was bright at the window and the snowflakes kept drifting down.

The owners of Northcote had stripped the great house of most of its furnishings. In particular, they had removed most of the paintings and furniture that had once graced the imposing rooms. One of the most daunting tasks facing Penny was replacing these.

'It's not like ordering curtains or deciding on the colour walls should be painted,' she told Ryan one morning over coffee. 'The art in a house like this is a collection, built up by different people over generations. It's very hard to replace that, especially in just a few months.'

'If anyone can do it, you can,' Ryan told her. 'You have a wonderful eye, Penny.'

She smiled at him. 'Oh, Ryan—you have such unbounded faith in my abilities.'

'You're an artist. I'm not. That was why you left me in the first place, wasn't it? Because I didn't let you spread your artistic wings wide enough?'

'Something like that,' she said with a grimace.

'Well, now you can spread them all you want,' he said. He looked at her over the rim of his coffee-cup, his grey eyes amused. 'This is building up to something. What?'

They were sitting in the projection room. It had just been completed, and was one of the few rooms in Northcote that held peace, being free of workmen and activity.

As a matter of fact, Penny loved this room, the only one Ryan himself had designed. She loved the maple panelling, the rich leather seats, the sumptuous carpeting. She loved the big screen and the surround speakers, which always gave her a tingle of anticipation, the same feeling she'd had as a child at her first movies.

It was the perfect place to screen films for select audiences, and it also made an elegant rendezvous in a house where almost every room was filled with strangers, so they had taken to meeting here for coffee and discussion. Nobody ever disturbed them here.

They were sitting in the back row, where the control panel was. Penny was going through her briefcase, Ryan checking his email on his laptop computer.

'Well,' Penny said, leaning back in the luxurious seat, 'you know I've been on the look-out for good quality pieces for Northcote?'

'Yes,' he said.

'I came across something quite exciting last week. There's going to be an auction sale at a country house in North Yorkshire next week. The place is called Havelock Hall, and it dates from the same period as Northcote. They have lots of exquisite things. In fact, it's a wonderful collection, all under one roof.'

'Sounds interesting,' he commented.

'I've been looking through the catalogue.' She opened her briefcase and passed him the auctioneer's catalogue, which was an inch thick. 'There are paintings, marbles, bronzes, clocks, carpets, silver, furniture, garden statuary—'

'Stop,' he laughed, flicking through the catalogue. 'I get the picture.'

'The house is being demolished, so everything has to be sold. One of the big London houses is doing the auction. The thing is, darling, it's a unique opportunity to pick up whole rooms-full of beautiful things that match. I could spend months buying pieces separately, but—'

'Hold on a moment,' he said, looking up from the catalogue. 'What?'

'Did you just call me "darling?"'

'No, you must have heard wrong.'

'I could have sworn you did.'

'Maybe some problem with the acoustics in here.'

'Maybe. Go on.'

She smiled at him. The truth was that they had been getting on so well lately that it frightened her and thrilled her at the same time. 'Well, it's a terrific opportunity. The only problem is—money. Together with what we've bought so far, we could furnish Northcote at practically one swoop from the Havelock collection. But it means a huge expenditure.'

Ryan nodded. 'And you want to know if I'm committed enough.'

'Yes.'

'I see you've marked several lots in this catalogue. Are these the pieces you're interested in?'

'Yes.' She leaned forward so she could point to some calculations she had made. 'They're all pieces in the same rooms. They go so perfectly together, do you see? My idea is we could transplant whole rooms from Havelock to Northcote. But to get the pieces we want, we might have to outbid some determined buyers. These are the auctioneer's estimates.'

Penny was leaning close to Ryan, and the silky drop of her hair was brushing his cheek.

'That perfume you're wearing is delicious,' he murmured, inhaling her scent. 'Is it new?'

'Yes, it's new. I found it on my bedside table. I think my fairy godmother must have left it there.'

'She has excellent taste.'

'Oh, she shops in Paris. At least, that's what the label says.'

Ryan touched the warm skin of her neck with his lips, sending shivers of pleasure down her spine. 'And how much would she have to spend to buy all these antiques you want?'

Penny reached over to the catalogue in his hands and flipped some pages. 'This is what I work out. I've calculated what we might have to spend using the high end of the estimate for each lot, in case we meet determined bidding.'

He looked at the figure. 'How many noughts is that?'

'It's horrendous, isn't it?' she agreed. 'But if we get lucky, we might spend much less than that. And even if we do pay the full amount, we'll be getting a marvellous collection at well below dealer prices.'

'So even if I spend this much, I'm actually saving money?'

'Got it. You should have been an economist.'

'And when is the sale?' His arm had somehow slipped round her waist and was drawing her close to him.

Penny rested her head on his broad shoulder and nestled close to him. 'Next Saturday.'

'Well, why don't we go up together?' He was trailing warm kisses across her closed eyelids and down the velvet of her cheeks towards her lips. 'North Yorkshire is beautiful.' He kissed the smiling corner of her mouth softly. 'Just like you.'

Penny's businesslike efficiency was dissolving under the tender onslaught. She lifted her chin so he could kiss her full on the lips. Ryan's tongue touched hers. She drew it into her mouth, feeling his hand slide into her shirt and cup the swell of her breast.

'What are you doing to me?' she whispered, her bones seeming to melt.

'We're making out in the back row of the movies,' he replied, deftly unfastening her bra.

'Shouldn't we wait until the lights go down?' she asked, looking up at him with drowning eyes.

'Your wish is my command, my darling.' He reached out and touched a switch on the control panel. The room lights dimmed into darkness.

And then she was lost in his arms.

CHAPTER TWELVE

THEY drove up to North Yorkshire on Friday in Ryan's sports car. The weather was bright and cold. As Ryan had predicted, the scenery was beautiful, not the sometimes bleak landscape of the moors, but a richly forested patchwork of little villages and green fields.

They took a suite at a hotel in the pretty market town of Barnard Castle. Havelock Hall was some ten miles' drive from Barnard Castle. It was a large house on more or less the same scale as Northcote, but in a very poor state of repair. As they walked to the hall through the ranks of other cars parked on the lawns—the auction was evidently drawing a lot of attention—there were obvious signs of neglect and decay.

'I hope the contents aren't as badly run-down as the house,' she said to Ryan, looking at the crumbling fabric of the once great building, 'or I'll have led us on a wild-goose chase!'

They signed in at the door and walked into the house.

'I don't think you need to worry,' Ryan said to her, looking around. 'These things are magnificent!'

It was true. The owners of Havelock Hall had collected splendid art works over the generations, and had clearly cherished their collection. As they walked from room to room,

Penny felt her pulses racing with excitement. It was a wonderland of desirable things, each bearing a numbered tag.

Here were sets of Sheraton and Hepplewhite furniture, perfectly in tune with the neoclassical style of Northcote; fine oil paintings from the late eighteenth to early twentieth centuries; Italian marbles and French bronzes; display cases filled with fine English china, collections of clocks, antique firearms, Persian carpets, Chinese and Indian *objects d'art*— rooms filled with beautiful objects that matched each other in that indefinable way that it took centuries to achieve.

'Oh, Ryan.' She grabbed his arm, her fingers biting into the hard muscles under his silk jacket. 'Those are the two paintings of the Lake District I told you about—they would look so wonderful in the dining room. And those exquisite marble busts are Florentine, late eighteenth century.'

'You should go on the *Antiques Roadshow*,' he smiled.

'I know there was a similar pair at Northcote, but the owners sold them years ago. I've seen pictures of them in a book about English country houses. These are just as good, if not better.'

'They are lovely things.'

'All the dealers are here,' Penny whispered to Ryan, looking around at the well-heeled viewers. 'Competition is going to be stiff!'

'How many noughts do I need to add to that figure you scribbled in the catalogue?' he asked wryly.

'Depends how serious you are about making Northcote into something truly special,' she replied.

'Hmm. Fighting talk. I'll tell you what. You can do the bidding tomorrow. If the price gets too rich for my blood, I'll nudge you in the ribs.'

She felt his biceps. 'God, you're so strong. Do you sneak off to the gym when I'm not looking?'

'I keep fit by punching Hollywood moguls in the nose.'

'Well, don't nudge too hard,' she commented, 'you might break one of my ribs.'

By midday on Saturday, when the auctioneer halted for lunch, she had bid successfully on two dozen lots, and Ryan had not prodded her in the ribs once.

Penny was in a state of euphoria. The things she had bought were so exquisite that she was as happy as though she had bought them for herself, rather than for Ryan.

'And we haven't had to really push the price once,' she exulted as they carried their paper plates to a quiet corner to eat. The lots for sale might be sublime, but the catering had only run to pies, sausage rolls and chips.

'I'm so relieved to see all the money we're saving,' Ryan said drily. 'That last pair of serpentine columns cost as much as a small car.'

'But when you see them at Northcote, with those alabaster figurines on them, you'll be glad you didn't stick me in the ribs!' She was exhilarated, bubbling. 'And we got those bronze garden statues! They just need to have the oxidation cleaned off, and then they'll be spectacular, on either side of our entrance hall.'

'Ask the tea-lady for a couple of mugs of this stuff,' he commented, wincing as he sipped his tea. 'It'd take the paint off a garden gnome.'

'You're right,' she said. 'We should have brought a bottle of champagne!' Eating quickly, she ran through her list. 'I can't believe we've got all these things, Ryan. We've done so well.'

'What else is on your list?' he asked.

'Poor baby,' she said, kissing him with a mouth flecked with flaky pastry, 'are you shell-shocked?'

'I'm just being dragged along behind your chariot,' he said with a smile. 'What are we going for this afternoon?'

'I've marked all sorts of things. But the lot I really want is this one.' She tapped the catalogue. 'The two paintings of the Lake District.'

Ryan glanced from the catalogue to the paintings in question, which stood by the auctioneer's rostrum, in preparation for the afternoon sale. They were very large, quite magnificent Victorian oil paintings, which made a matching pair, in heavy gilt frames. 'The one on the left looks like Grasmere,' Penny said, 'with the mountains in the background. The other one might be Coniston, with the islands in the lake. They're both very beautiful.'

'They could be very valuable, too. The work is as good as early Constable, though they're unsigned. I'd be prepared to bet that, with a little research, they'll turn out to be by a major artist.'

'I love them,' Ryan said. 'Whoever painted them was a master.'

'There might be a lot of competition for them. The price could go way past the estimate.'

'Why do you say that?'

'See those two?' She pointed to a very expensively dressed couple who were standing near the big landscapes. 'They're London dealers. They keep going to look at the paintings. I know they're going to bid for them.'

'They look as though they mean business.'

'So do I.' She glared at the dealers through narrowed, amethyst eyes. 'That blonde hair isn't real. *And* she's had a face-lift.'

Ryan was watching her with a smile. 'If you glare at them like that, they'll catch fire.'

'Are you laughing at me?' she demanded.

'No. I'm just filled with admiration. I didn't know you had so much nerve. I'm seeing a new side of you today.'

'Scary, isn't it?' she giggled.

'Impressive, I would say.'

'Did you think I could spend your money this fast?' The tension and excitement of the morning were fizzing inside Penny—she really didn't need champagne. In a few hours she had purchased wonderful things for Northcote. Her hunch was proving to have been an inspiration. 'I'm so pleased with myself!'

'I can see that. Well, I hope you get your lake paintings. Those two seem to have plenty of money.'

'You're not going to dig me in the ribs, are you?' she demanded. 'I really, *really* have to have those paintings.'

'We'll have to see,' he grinned. 'Maybe my nerve will give way. I'm probably not as brave as you.'

'You are so cruel. I want those oil paintings,' she told Ryan. 'They're masterpieces. I'm sorry to be so obsessed. You'd think I was buying them for myself.'

'I hope you are,' he murmured.

'What do you mean?' Penny asked.

He paused before answering. 'Northcote is your home if you want it. You know that.'

She met his eyes, and felt her heart turn over in her breast. 'Let's just get through the auction,' she replied awkwardly.

'I offered to marry you last year. I want you more than ever now. You are buying these things for yourself—and Northcote belongs to you—as far as I'm concerned.'

'They would be wonderful in the dining room,' she said distractedly, trying to ignore what his words were doing to her. 'One on each side.'

'I love your breasts,' he said.

'What?' she blinked.

'They're masterpieces, too. And there's one on each side. I want them in my bedroom. Forever.'

'Do you ever stop thinking about sex?' she demanded.

'No. It's too wonderful for me to ever forget. Do you?'

She was spared having to answer by the arrival of the auctioneer and his assistants. The sale was about to recommence. The bidders were all resuming their seats, so Penny and Ryan followed suit.

Each bidder had been issued with a number card. Theirs was number thirteen, which had proved to be lucky so far. She hoped their luck would hold this afternoon. She was tense with anticipation as the first lots were brought up and quickly auctioned off. Ryan's words were echoing in her head.

When he had last offered to marry her, she'd been pregnant. He was doing 'the right thing'—or that was what she had assumed. If she hadn't lost the baby, she suddenly thought, she would probably have gone back to him.

After all, her plan to soldier on through university and a part-time job, with a baby on her hip, would have been very tough to carry through. In the end she would probably have gone back to him. By now he would have been her husband.

That thought had never occurred to her before, and it made her feel very strange. She was lost in thought for a long while.

Ryan nudged her gently.

'I'm not bidding for anything,' she whispered.

'Maybe you should be,' he replied.

She looked up and saw that the two big landscapes were on the rostrum. Bidding had already started, and was well underway. She saw the flash of a card—number fifty-seven—in the hands of the peroxide-blonde antiques dealer.

Her heart pounding, Penny held up her own card, and saw the auctioneer's eyes glance at her.

'I have twenty-five thousand from the lady to my right,' she heard him tell the room. 'Twenty-five thousand pounds. Any advance on twenty-five?'

Penny felt her stomach drop down to her feet. She'd been

so busy thinking about Ryan that she hadn't even noticed the bidding! At that price, the paintings had already far exceeded the auctioneer's top estimate. And already, the blonde woman was lifting her card.

'Twenty-six,' the auctioneer intoned, 'thank you, madam. I have twenty-seven at the back of the room. Twenty-eight at the front. Twenty-nine at the back. Against you, madam.'

Her mouth dry, Penny looked over her shoulder to see who the bidder at the back was. She caught sight of a raised card—number ninety-two, in the hands of a distinguished-looking Chinese man.

At thirty thousand pounds, the bidding paused. The blonde woman at the front had the bid. Penny tipped her card to the auctioneer.

'Thank you, madam,' he said, 'thirty-one thousand. Thirty-two. Thirty-three. Thirty-four.'

Penny was breathless. The Chinese man and the two London dealers were bidding against each other fast. She glanced at Ryan. He seemed completely relaxed, his grey eyes hooded as he followed the action. If he could have bought a small car for the price of the serpentine columns, he could buy a very big one for this price. But he seemed unperturbed.

At forty thousand, the bidding hesitated.

Penny lifted her card again.

'Forty-one thousand,' the auctioneer said, smiling at her, 'thank you, madam. Any advance on forty-one thousand for this magnificent pair of oil paintings?'

There was a *frisson* of interest through the room. She and Ryan always attracted attention when they were together, because they were such a striking couple, and today she had bid successfully on a number of keenly contested lots. There were smiles and nods directed her way.

But not from the blonde woman in the front row. She turned and glared at Penny over her shoulder for a moment. Then she waved her card imperiously.

'Forty-two in the front row,' the auctioneer said unctuously. 'Thank *you*, madam. Forty-three at the back. Forty-four. Forty-five, thank you, sir. Forty-six. Forty-seven.'

It was going up frighteningly fast. Penny found herself gripping Ryan's hand. She was shaking with tension. 'What should I do?' she hissed.

'It's up to you,' he murmured calmly.

Muttering a prayer that this would clinch it, she lifted her card.

'Forty-eight, on my right,' the auctioneer noted.

The blonde woman gave Penny another ferocious scowl, and waggled her card.

'Forty-nine. Forty-nine thousand pounds.'

Penny's nails dug into Ryan's hand. She looked at him. He neither nodded nor shook his head.

Penny lifted her card. It felt as heavy as a block of lead.

'Fifty thousand pounds,' said the auctioneer. There was a ripple of applause around the room. The blonde woman and her husband both turned to glare at Penny. The man's face, which was thin and pale, was shiny with perspiration. He dabbed his brow with a handkerchief.

His partner jabbed her card in the air defiantly.

'Fifty-one,' the auctioneer declared. 'Fifty-two at the back. Fifty-three. Fifty-four.'

Penny wanted to throw up. They were bidding at twice the estimate. Was she digging a very big hole for herself?

She looked at the two paintings. They were the finest landscapes she had ever seen outside of a museum. They were perfect for Northcote. And whatever they cost now, she would probably never get a chance like this again.

She lifted her card.

'Thank you, madam, I have fifty-five thousand on my right. Any advance?'

The blonde woman, looking as though she were sucking on a lemon, brandished her card.

'Fifty-six, thank you. Fifty-seven at the back. Fifty-eight in the front. Fifty-nine at the back.'

Once again, the bidding faltered. The room was buzzing with electricity. It was a lot of money. But Penny was aware of an odd phenomenon. Beyond her tightly coiled nerves, she felt that the two paintings were looking more beautiful with each raise in the bidding.

She suddenly felt, with a calm certainty, that these two magnificent works were worth every penny, and much more.

She glanced at Ryan. He merely smiled at her. 'Your call,' he said quietly.

Penny raised her card.

Through the applause, she heard the auctioneer intone, 'I am bid sixty thousand by the lady on my right. Any advance on sixty thousand?'

The blonde woman thrust her card into the air.

'Sixty-one in the front row,' the auctioneer said, looking enquiringly at Penny. 'Against you, madam.'

Penny's arm was too shaky to lift the card, so she simply nodded.

'Thank you, madam. I have sixty-two thousand pounds on my right. Any advance?'

This time, the blonde woman did not move, but sat with shoulders hunched in defeat.

Penny could not help turning to look at the Asian man at the back. He caught her eye and smiled, but shook his head to indicate he would not bid.

There was absolute silence among the crowd as the auctioneer repeated the final bid, his gavel poised in his hand.

When he rapped the hammer onto the lectern, there was a rush of clapping and excited talk. Penny slumped against Ryan, her head lolling on his shoulder.

'Please say you forgive me,' she said in his ear.

'I'm proud of you,' he whispered. 'I love you, Penny Bun. Well done!'

'Oh, Ryan!'

His strong arms came around her, and he hugged her hard. 'Are there many more lots on your list?' he asked.

'No, why?'

'Because I can't wait to get you home—and into bed,' he grinned.

Ryan was usually so tender with her after their lovemaking, kissing her gently, telling her how exquisite, how desirable she was, making her feel like the most beautiful woman in the world. That night, in their hotel room, although he held her and kissed her, he was unusually silent.

At last he spoke quietly.

'It's time you fulfilled the other part of your promise, darling.'

'What do you mean?' she asked sleepily.

'You should have that check-up, Penny.'

She groaned. 'But I'm fine! I don't need to see any doctors!'

'You should have been for a check-up every few months,' he said, stroking her hair. 'You can't keep running away from things.'

'I don't run away from things,' she retorted.

Ryan smiled. 'You are the perfect woman. Almost. About the only fault you have is…that you run away from things. Now, why don't we do it this week?'

'You can't just pitch up at a neurologist's office,' she said. 'You have to make an appointment and they're always booked up for months in advance.'

'Dr Brent-Jones will see you at a moment's notice,' Ryan replied. 'He's very concerned about you. There won't be any wait, I promise you that. I'll call him and make an appointment when we get back to Northcote. We can drive to Exeter together, if you like. Spend a couple of days in Devon. Make a break of it.'

'You're coming with me?' she asked suspiciously, raising her tousled head so she could look at him.

'Yes,' he replied firmly. 'No negotiation on this one, Penny Bun.'

She sighed, sinking back down into his arms. 'Oh, hell. I suppose Ariadne can manage without me for a few days, if we get Tara in full-time.'

'You can shut the damned shop for all I care,' he retorted, with a return to his old imperious ways. 'We're talking about your health here, Penny!'

'All right,' Penny sighed, capitulating, 'if it will stop you from bullying me.'

'Good,' he said. 'We'll call Brent-Jones on Monday morning.' Ryan kissed her throat softly. 'I hope I haven't tired you out? The night is yet young, my beloved!'

CHAPTER THIRTEEN

THE snowfalls had been, if anything, even heavier in the west. It was noon by the time they got to Devon, less than a week later, and the winter sun gleamed fitfully on huge banks of snow by the sides of the roads. There was no sign of a thaw. Indeed, the mass of dark clouds from the sea promised yet more snow soon.

The drive had been beautiful, despite the slushy roads. Ryan had chosen the luxurious Land Cruiser for the poor driving conditions, and they had avoided the crowded motorways, choosing more scenic, less busy routes.

Snuggled into the opulent leather seat, Penny had been enjoying the drive, luxuriating in Ryan's relaxed company, enchanted by the snowy landscapes of Surrey, Hampshire and Wiltshire that they drove through. There was something so safe about watching such a cold world pass by, secure in the big car, with Ryan at the wheel.

Ryan's suggestion that they spend a couple of days in Devon had turned into a necessity—Brent-Jones had ordered a brain scan for today, and wanted to see her tomorrow, when he had had a chance to examine the results. She was not looking forward to either the scan or the interview.

They reached their hotel, the Angler's Retreat, a beautiful

country inn outside Exeter. After unpacking and stretching their
legs, they went to the restaurant for a light lunch. It was a
charming room, with Tudor timbered ceilings and walls, and a
welcoming fire in the big, farmhouse fireplace. The walls were
decorated with antique rods, nets and other fishing paraphernalia.

The waiter had just brought their food when Ryan's cellphone rang. He answered the call, spoke briefly, then snapped
the phone shut.

'That was the real-estate people in Tunbridge Wells. The
owners of Northcote have accepted my offer.'

'Oh, Ryan!' she exclaimed, feeling butterflies in her
stomach. 'So it's yours!'

'It will be when I've parted with a sizeable chunk of cash,'
he replied. His grey eyes held hers. 'I committed myself a long
time ago, Penny. We're going to make it beautiful. We're
going to make it live again.'

The waiter served their grilled trout and they started eating,
talking about Northcote Hall and the beautiful new things they
had bought in Yorkshire, which were due to be delivered the
following week. Penny was nervous and excited about the
arrival of her treasures.

'You really need to employ a full-time gardener,' she told
Ryan. 'There's already a perfect kitchen garden at the back.
And with a little greenhouse, we could have our own fresh
vegetables and salads all year long.'

'You're right, we could,' he smiled.

Her appointment with the scanner was not until three that afternoon. They had time to have a leisurely meal. Though Penny
did not for one moment feel that there was anything organically
wrong with her, she was dreading her return to St Cyprian's.

She must have shown some of the strain in her face,
because Ryan touched her hand.

'Are you nervous about this afternoon?' he asked.

'Not about the check-up,' she replied. 'I'm just not looking forward to being in St Cyprian's again. The place has…' She stopped short.

'Very painful associations for you?' he finished.

'Yes. And the scanner isn't very nice. It's noisy and claustrophobic.'

Ryan kissed her gently on the cheek. 'I'll be with you this afternoon,' he promised. 'In fact, I promise never to let you come to a hospital alone again.'

Penny tried to make a meal of the delicious grilled trout, but her appetite seemed to have vanished. They went back to their room and lay on the bed, wrapped in one another's arms without speaking, until it was time to go to the hospital.

St Cyprian's was a large Victorian hospital with a rather forbidding air, half-cloister and half-prison. The facilities behind the grim granite façade, however, were modern and clinical.

The surroundings were all too familiar to Penny, and she found herself gripping Ryan's hand so hard that she must have hurt him, though he gave no sign. Their first appointment, before seeing Dr Brent-Jones the next day, was at the radiology unit.

The huge scanning machine had always intimidated her, and she wished Ryan could be there with her. But here she had to say goodbye to him. It did help, however, to know that he was just in the next room, and that if panic overwhelmed her she could run to him. It also helped to hear his voice in her head, promising she would never need to come to a hospital on her own again.

She lay perfectly still, as the technician ordered her—by now, she knew the drill well. The machine slid her into its maw. Though she was not claustrophobic by nature, it was not pleasant to lie in such a confined space. The great curved shell of the gantry was somehow threatening. She kept her eyes closed, and tried not to flinch when the scan began.

The noise was repetitive, harsh and loud, and as always Penny was reminded of some huge butchering apparatus that was taking slices out of her. Of course, the slices were only virtual, and there was no pain. But the ugly hammering sound brought everything back with frightening clarity.

She lay motionless, remembering the pain of it all—the physical pain in her head and neck that had seemed to be crushing her. The emotional pain of knowing that she was no longer going to be a mother, that it was all over.

And, as always, she could not stop herself from remembering the night her father had died, the agonisingly long wait, the final glimpse of his broken body.

She felt dazed and shaky when the scan finally ended. She tried to put a brave face on it, but Ryan took one look at her and gathered her in his arms. If she hadn't stopped him, he would have carried her out of St Cyprian's like a child. As it was, he kept an arm tight around her waist to help her walk.

He drove her swiftly back to the Angler's Retreat. By now it was getting dark, and the snow that had been threatening all day had started to fall—big white stars like something on a Christmas tree. Indeed, it would not be long before Christmas was here. The streets of Exeter were gay with lights and decorations and the streets had that peculiar happy bustle of Christmas.

Her legs were still shaky when they got out of the Land Cruiser.

'We'll have Room Service send us up something to eat,' Ryan said firmly. 'It's an early night for you, Penny Bun.'

Their room was deliciously warm and cosy. Penny took a hot bath, as Ryan commanded. Lying in the foamy bubbles, she started to feel much more relaxed. Ryan came to sit with her and talk about the day. He brought her a whisky on the rocks, which she drank gratefully. He was handsomer than ever, the rugged bone structure of his face emphasised by the weight he had lost. He had never put it back on. The sleekness she had known in London seemed to have gone forever—it seemed to have disappeared along with that infuriating arrogance. What remained was a quieter self-confidence, strengthened by a willingness to listen.

'Was it as bad as you expected?' he asked her.

'It brought back memories, more than anything,' she told him.

'Is your neck sore?'

She smiled up at him. 'How did you know?'

He pushed up the sleeves of his black sweater and began to massage her neck and shoulders. His fingers were strong and expert, bringing deep relief.

'I've bought you a little present,' he told her as she groaned with pleasure at the expertise of his kneading hands.

'Not more jewels,' she protested.

Ryan laughed. 'No, something much more mundane, I'm afraid. I'll give it to you when I've finished your massage.'

It was delicious to let Ryan pamper her. When the tension in her shoulders had quite gone, he wrapped her in a towel and led her to the bedroom. 'Here,' he said, giving her a tissue-wrapped parcel. 'To keep you warm.'

Penny unwrapped the gift, and could not help smiling. It was an exquisite pair of pyjamas, pale blue with pink sheep dotted all over. 'They're adorable,' she said, kissing him. 'Thank you, darling.'

'Put them on,' he commanded, 'and let's get into bed.'

She slipped into the pyjamas, delighting in the feel of the soft silk on her skin. 'Did you know that "pyjamas" is one of my favourite words?' she said. 'It must be a Chinese word.'

'As a matter of fact, it's Persian,' he told her solemnly. 'From two Urdu words, *pa* and *jama*, meaning "sexy love-pants".'

'You know so much,' she giggled.

'Especially about pyjamas,' he agreed, undressing. He always slept in the nude, and Penny was privately certain that it was part of the reason why they made love so much. It was impossible to lie next to that magnificent naked male body and not find her thoughts straying.

Tonight she felt tired and jangled, though. She doubted whether they would be making the bedsprings of the Angler's Retreat squeak tonight.

They slipped into bed and pulled the covers over them. Ryan pulled her close to him and laid her head on his chest. 'I know today has been a strain,' he murmured, stroking her tenderly. 'Is that why you never went back for your check-ups? Because you dreaded being back in a place where you suffered so much?'

'That's partly why,' she confessed. 'I've never been very good with hospitals in the first place. It started when I was ten. When my father had his accident.'

'Tell me about it,' Ryan said gently.

She shrugged painfully. 'There isn't much to tell. He was coming home from work. There was a bad accident just two streets away from our house. He was taken to hospital in an ambulance. The police came to call us. My mother and I rushed to the hospital. They wouldn't let us see him, though.'

'Was he in theatre?' Ryan asked quietly.

Penny nodded, reliving the anguish of that terrible evening. 'They tried to save his life, but he had been too badly injured. We waited for six hours outside the intensive-care unit. At midnight they came out and told us he had died. They let us go in to see him. It was only for a moment.' Her eyes were wet with tears. 'Hardly even time to realise that he was dead. Ever since then, whenever I go into a hospital, I feel sick and dizzy. Something about the smells and sounds, I suppose, must bring it all back.'

'You've never told me any of this before,' Ryan said, kissing away her tears.

She shook her head. 'I know. Then last year—the encephalitis, the miscarriage—gave me another reason to hate hospitals. They don't have very good associations for me, I'm afraid.'

'I understand. Sleep, now, my darling. Tomorrow everything will be all right.'

He put Penny on her side and snuggled into her back, holding her close. She lay cradled in his arms, so grateful for his warmth. 'It's so strange to be back in Devonshire,' she said with a sigh. 'I'm glad you're here with me.'

'Me, too.'

Ryan was kissing the back of her neck, nuzzling in the fragrant auburn curls. It was deliciously erotic. She arched gently.

Ryan's arms were so strong and supportive. He held her close. One of his hands slid into her pyjama top, caressing her soft breasts, teasing the sensitive nipples into life. The other slipped into her pyjama bottom, stroking her abdomen, invading the triangle of feminine curls at her loins.

'Why, Mr Wolfe,' she murmured, 'what *are* you doing?'

'I'm taking your pyjamas for a test drive,' he said, his breath warm and sexy in her ear.

She giggled softly. She was too relaxed and happy to do anything but concentrate on the sheer pleasure he gave her. Within moments, she was moaning in ecstasy as he cupped both her breasts with one hand while the other glided across the liquid smoothness of her loins.

'I love you,' he whispered, his fingers dipping inside her to make her gasp out loud. 'You're the most beautiful woman in the world, and I will desire you till the day I die.'

Waves of delight spread through her tired body, shocking in their intensity, until the biggest and strongest wave of all rolled her up in a ball of pleasure and had her whimpering his name, not knowing whether she wanted him to stop, or keep on forever.

She reached behind her and felt his intense arousal against her. 'I want you,' she whispered.

'Don't move.' He slipped her pyjama bottoms down to her knees and then took her in his arms again. He covered her neck and face with kisses as he made love to her, his desire filling her, exciting her, taking away all fear and pain. With him inside her like this, big and solid and male, it was impossible to feel anything but joy.

He loved her with exquisite gentleness until their climax locked them into a quivering knot, holding them unbearably tight.

Then Penny felt herself slipping into sleep as though into the depths of a dark sea.

This time, their destination at St Cyprian's was the neurology unit.

After a brief wait in the reception area, they were sent into Dr Brent-Jones's office.

Ellis Brent-Jones was a respected doctor in his field. Now close to seventy, he looked fit and tanned, his white hair and beard cropped close to his narrow head. His piercing blue eyes lit up as he saw Penny walk into his office.

'Ah, Miss Watkins,' he chirped. 'The prodigal returns!'

After she had left Ryan in London, she had started using her stepfather's name, Watkins, instead of her born name, Wellcome. She had seen no reason to change it back—it had helped make it hard for Ryan to trace her, even with all the money and power at his disposal.

'Hello, Dr Brent-Jones,' she said, shaking hands with him. 'I'm sorry I never came back to thank you for all you did for me.'

'Hardly the point,' he said with asperity. 'Your health is the real question, young lady—especially since your fiancé informs me you took yourself off the medication I prescribed without consulting a doctor!'

Penny gave Ryan a sharp look at the word *fiancé* before replying. 'I'm sorry about that, too, but the pills made me feel awful. I hated taking them.'

'Well, let's just be grateful that you've decided to come and see me at last,' the doctor said. 'I have the results of your scan here. I want to perform some simple tests, and then we can speak.'

The next forty minutes were not exactly comfortable for Penny, as the specialist subjected her to a minute process of pricking, prodding and tapping with a rubber hammer, designed—or so she presumed—to check that her neurological responses were all intact.

Ryan waited outside through this indignity, much to her relief, after which Brent-Jones asked her a battery of questions, noting all her answers in tiny writing in her file.

Apparently satisfied at last, the specialist put down his pen and called Ryan back into the office. He sat beside her, taking her hand comfortingly. Brent-Jones looked at them both keenly.

'The scan results are very encouraging. The damage done by the encephalitis appears to be minimal, and there has been good healing.'

Ryan squeezed her fingers tightly. The specialist went on, 'The biggest danger for you, Penny, after your brain inflammation, is the possibility of what we call temporal lobe epilepsy. The symptoms vary greatly, but they can be unpleasant and even dangerous. That's why I prescribed that medication. You took a most unwarranted risk when you stopped taking it. What if you had blacked out while driving a car, eh? What if you had injured yourself—or your passengers—or innocent people in another vehicle?'

'You're right,' Penny said in a small voice. 'I've been a fool.'

'Well, the good news is that there seems to be no sign of anything like that. You seem to have been very lucky. I would prefer that you went back on the medication for another year, just to be sure. But, considering that the side-effects you describe are so severe, I'm going to recommend that you try some alternative means of preventing the possibility of any problems. There are a range of holistic treatments that can be effective, and I want you to try them. I also want you to go to a neurologist for a proper check-up every four months. There are excellent people in Tunbridge Wells, and I'm going to refer you to more than one, so you can take your pick.'

He scribbled some names and numbers on a pad. Ryan squeezed her hand and gave her a quick smile. She could see the relief in his beautiful eyes.

'About the other thing—your losing your baby, I mean,' the doctor continued, 'you shouldn't be too concerned about any problems in that department. There was no damage to the reproductive system, and from what you tell me, everything is quite normal in that respect. Any time you want to try for another baby, you can go right ahead.'

'Thanks,' Penny said, flushing to the roots of her hair.

After a short talk about alternative therapies, Brent-Jones gave Penny a thick wad of material to read on the subject. Warmer than when he had first greeted her—he, too, was evidently greatly relieved at his findings—he ushered them out.

They said their thanks and goodbyes in the reception area. As the doctor walked away, his secretary called to Penny.

'Miss Watkins? I've got a note for you here from the porters' office—you left some things here when you checked out last year. They've been kept for you all this time, if you'd like to pick them up.'

'Oh, thank you. I wonder what they can be?'

The secretary explained how to get to the lost property office, and Penny and Ryan walked there. Their route took them along one of the cloister-like passages that bounded the central gardens, now piled with dirty snow, and not very beautiful.

'I'm so relieved,' Ryan said, stopping to hug her hard enough to squeeze the breath out of her body for a moment. 'What did he do to you while I was out?'

'If you like, I'll show you when we get back to the hotel,' she replied meaningfully. 'It involved a thing with a sharp point at one end and a rubber hammer at the other!'

'Hmm, too kinky for me,' Ryan grinned. 'The main thing is he seems happy with the results. You ought to have changed your first name, too, baby doll—to Lucky!'

They reached the porters' office and a pleasant Sikh went into the store room with the ticket the secretary had given Penny. He returned with a clear plastic bag which contained a few items of clothing, a book, the red cellphone, and what looked like an envelope.

Through the plastic, she could see that on the address side were written only the two words 'Ryan Wolfe'.

She stared at it blankly for a moment.

'Oh, Ryan,' she said. 'It's the letter I wrote you.'

'Letter?' he repeated.

'I told you—I wrote to you when they discharged me. Telling you what had happened.'

'Why is it still here?'

She stared at the envelope blankly. 'I was so confused. My brain wasn't really working. I was having hallucinations and delusions. I must have thought that I had posted it. Or perhaps I meant to fill the address in when I got home—but I must have left it here. That's where it's been all this time. That's why I never posted it.'

He stared at her with a strange expression. 'Can I read it?' he asked quietly.

'I don't know!' She held the bag protectively in her arms. 'Not here, anyway, and not now!'

'OK.' With something of his old grimness of manner, he took her arm. 'Let's go.'

They got into the Land Cruiser. Penny was still holding the plastic bag tight against her breasts.

'Where do you want to go?' Ryan asked her.

She closed her eyes. 'Anywhere. I don't mind.'

'We'll take a drive,' he decided, 'then look for somewhere to have lunch.'

Out of the city of Exeter, the roads were still slushy with snow. Thick white drifts had levelled out the hollows and bumps of the Devon landscape, making everything look surreal. Ryan drove carefully, concentrating on the roads, and she stared out of the window, barely recognising the landscape that should have been so familiar to her. After all, it was around here that she had grown up.

Finding this parcel, with the letter she had written and never posted almost a year ago, had changed her mood. Emotions that she did not even want to recognise were perilously close to the surface now.

Finally, she realised that they were driving onto Dartmoor, and had reached a part of the countryside that she recognised. The high, wild country near Okehampton had a special meaning for her. It was here that she had walked with Tom, when he'd first had her in his sights. These bleak granitic hills had been where he'd started his campaign of seduction with her.

That had been long before she'd known that he had done it all before, with other clever, pretty students before her—

quoting the same poetry, bringing the same bottle of champagne out of his rucksack, making her feel so special...

The area, always sombre, was now carpeted in snow. Only where strata of rock lifted themselves up out of the moor, like ancient trolls trying to emerge from underground prisons, was there any contrast to the smooth white contours.

Penny looked at Ryan, wondering why he had brought her here, whether he knew that this place had associations for her. He caught her glance and smiled slightly.

'You see, I do listen to what you tell me.'

'I told you about this place?'

'You said that this was where you and Tom walked, that summer. Where you and he became lovers.'

'You remembered that,' she said, looking around her with deep violet eyes. 'Of all the things I told you, you remembered that.'

'As a matter of fact, I remember every word you've ever said to me,' he said. 'Though you obviously don't believe that.'

'Why did you bring me here?' she asked, shivering despite the warmth of the car.

'I wanted to see the place,' he replied.

'You mean you wanted to make me confront my ghosts!' she retorted.

Ryan's grey eyes glittered for a moment. 'You've been doing so well so far. You've confronted two already today.'

'I hate you sometimes,' she said, glaring at him. Then her gaze was drawn to the wild hills and the dark clouds that lowered menacingly over them. 'It was summer then,' she said quietly. 'It didn't look like this. The skies were blue. The moor was green and covered with flowers. It was wild and beautiful.'

Ryan parked the car at the side of the road, leaving the engine running so they would stay warm. 'Why did you come here, in particular?'

'It was Tom's idea. He loved romantic places like this.' The emphasis she put on the word *romantic* was bitter. Tom had chosen places like this because they put young women in the right frame of mind—not because he was a nature-lover. 'He was chairman of the hiking club at Varsity. If he didn't find a suitable girl in his class, chances were always good he would find one in the hiking club.'

'A suitable girl?'

'There was usually a new one each year,' she said in a flat voice. 'Sometimes they lasted longer.'

'I sometimes wonder how he managed to seduce so many,' Ryan said. 'He's not handsome, or impressive in any way.'

Penny looked at him in surprise. 'You've seen him?' she asked.

'I met him.'

'How did you achieve that?'

Ryan replied with a shrug. 'It wasn't hard. Little men with large egos are very easy to manipulate. I told him I admired his books. He was most eager to meet me.'

'You are so machiavellian it frightens me,' she gasped, looking at him with wide eyes.

'So what was his secret?' Ryan asked with that slight smile.

'No big secret, darling,' she said, shaking her head. 'He just chose very innocent, very gullible young women—and said exactly the right things to them.'

'Were you a virgin?' Ryan asked, stroking her hair.

'In every way. Mentally, spiritually, sexually. A silly girl, looking for a father figure. I was such easy prey for Tom. Just what he liked. He liked them tender. Didn't like to have to do too much chewing.'

'I'm sure he had never seen anyone as exquisite as you,' Ryan said gently.

'Well, that's what he told me,' she said drily. 'We walked

from here to Yes Tor. When we got there, it felt as if we had reached the top of the world. It was like being part of the sky. Tom opened his rucksack and brought out a bottle of champagne and a blanket. He quoted Shakespeare sonnets to me. Like I said, basic but effective. It was so easy for him.'

'Were you in love with him?' Ryan asked.

'Of course I thought I was.'

'Did you think he loved you?'

'Yes. At first, anyway. Later, I knew he couldn't possibly love me.'

'Why?'

'Because of the way he made love. He was so intent on getting what he wanted. You know the way some people eat, just grabbing handfuls and stuffing it into their mouths? That's what he was like. I didn't know much about sex, my love, but I knew that it wasn't the way it was meant to be. I knew I shouldn't feel… violated every time.'

'My poor baby,' he said quietly. 'I'm so sorry.'

'Don't be. You showed me how wonderful sex could be. You taught me how to love and be loved. You always made me feel like the most beautiful woman in the world. Tom wanted to degrade me. He loved control, more than anything else. He wanted you to know that you were in his power—in every way. He was my tutor, and when I tried to break up with him, he made it clear that I wasn't going to pass my exams unless I did exactly what he wanted. I was trapped.'

A group of shaggy Aberdeen Angus cattle moved slowly past the Land Cruiser, nosing through the snow for something to graze on. Only the hardiest animals could survive up here.

'Did you try to tell anyone what was happening?' Ryan asked.

'I was too much under Tom's spell,' she replied. 'You have to understand that I was so naive. I was just a timid first-year student. He was a professor, the author of textbooks, much older than me—and he held all the cards. No matter how badly he behaved, I kept telling myself that he was a genius, that I must be wrong about him. So I never told anyone. Not even my mother. I just grew very, very unhappy.'

'Did you pass your exams?'

'Oh, with flying colours.' Penny grimaced. 'At the top of the class. The trouble is, I knew I didn't deserve the high marks I got. I didn't do any work. I couldn't. I was too miserable to open a book. The marks were my reward for being in Tom's bed. Other students knew what was happening, and they said things. They were angry because I did better than any of them—even the ones who really worked for it.'

'People know about Tom,' Ryan said. 'I've made enquiries. He's wrecked a lot of students' careers—and lives, in some cases.'

'Oh, yes,' she replied, her beautiful mouth twisting. 'People in the faculty know about Tom—but nobody does anything, Ryan. He's too respected.'

'That may change, one day,' Ryan said quietly.

'I doubt it. Famous professors who publish trendy books are practically bulletproof, my dear.'

'True,' he agreed. 'What happened in your second year?'

'Looking back,' she said slowly, 'I suppose I had a nervous breakdown. It all just went on too long for me. It was Aubrey who rescued me—my stepfather. He came down and took me away. I couldn't study any more, anyway. I would never have got through my second-year exams. I was just crying all the time.' She shuddered as she remembered that awful time. 'So I came to London to find a job.'

'And met me,' he said.

'And met you,' she agreed. 'I'd been in London less than a year when I met you.'

Ryan was watching her with intelligent eyes. 'Hmm. Out of the frying pan and into the fire, some might say.'

She smiled at him. 'Some might say that, yes.' She reached for the plastic packet the porter had given her and took out the envelope. 'Ryan, I don't know what I wrote in this letter. I can't remember. But I wrote it for you, and you never received it. When I didn't hear from you again, I assumed you just couldn't forgive me for what I had done. I thought your silence was your answer. I was so hurt that I deliberately hid myself in case you ever changed your mind! I'm sorry it happened that way. I didn't mean to leave you dangling all this time. Whatever is in this letter, maybe it will explain how I felt, and why I did what I did. Maybe it's just silly nonsense. But either way, I want you to have it.'

She passed Ryan the letter. He took it, his eyes never leaving hers. 'Thank you. It means a lot to me to know that you wrote to me. Even if it is silly nonsense.'

He opened the envelope and took out the letter.

CHAPTER FOURTEEN

PENNY stared out of the window, her eyes drifting across the snowbound landscape, while Ryan read the letter. She did not know what the letter contained. All she remembered was that what she had wanted to say to him then had been overwhelmingly important to her, yet, by some quirk of fate, he had never received it.

He finished reading the letter, and turned to look at her.

'What are you thinking?' he asked her.

'Oh...I was just replaying my life,' she told him. 'I was remembering that day with Tom, when it all started. The eighteen months of misery that followed. The way I ran to London, like Dick Whittington. The first time I set eyes on you, and knew that you were someone very special in my life.'

'I remember that day, too,' he said gently.

'It was so overwhelmingly strange to enter your world, Ryan. The way you live is so magical, so different from anything I've ever known. I remember how I felt, that first time you made love to me, in Mexico. Do you have any idea what a revelation that was for a woman who had never dreamed that physical love could be anything like that?'

'It was a revelation to me, too. I never knew what it was like to love like that, either.'

'I remember Milan so vividly. How things started to fall apart when we got back. The way I panicked when I finally had to accept that I was pregnant. How sick I felt as I ran back to Exeter. The feeling of being swallowed up by the encephalitis, and being spat out a fortnight later, weak and forlorn.

'And I remember how you arrived one cold, bright morning and opened my door again. Ryan, it's taken me weeks to realise that you were opening my door to another chance. Another shot at happiness. That impossibly rare chance to start again, and this time make it work.'

'And do you think it is working?' he asked her.

'Yes, I do think it's working,' she said. Their eyes met. 'It's not *just* working for me, Ryan,' she said quietly. 'These past weeks, I've been happier than I ever believed possible— happier than I ever deserved to be. It has taken me all this time to begin to understand who you are.'

He smiled at her. 'And who am I?' he asked.

'Lucinda once told me that you were a very special man,' she said. 'She called you a magician. She said that you made wonderful things happen. That's all true. But you're much more than that. You're the man who loves me.'

'Yes,' Ryan said, 'I am.'

'And I'm the woman who loves you,' she went on. 'I hope you can forgive me for all my silliness and confusion. I hope you can forgive me for the way I've hurt you.'

'Penny, I hope you can forgive me for trying to bulldoze you into loving me. That was unforgivable. You gave me a second chance, too. A second chance to see just what a precious, what a wonderful person you are.'

She felt a hot lump in her throat. She swallowed, but it would not go down. 'What does the letter say?' she asked him. 'Is it silly nonsense?'

'Read it,' he said, passing her the sheets, 'judge for yourself.'

Penny took the letter from his fingers. She recognised her own handwriting. In places the lines were weak and rambling, ending in blots or confused scratchings-out. In others the words were regular and measured.

My darling Ryan,

I am writing to you from St Cyprian's Hospital, in Exeter. I've been here for two weeks. When I left you in London, I was already sick with encephalitis, a brain inflammation. Though I did not know it, I was very ill. For several days I was in a coma. When I came out of it, they told me that I had lost our baby.

Ryan, I am so sorry to give you this sad news. I know how happy you were when I told you we were going to have a child. And, although I seemed to hate the thought, deep inside I wanted your baby so much.

I feel so desolate. I am like a tree which has been stripped of all its leaves. I don't know if I will ever recover. Right now, it seems to me that I was a being who lived in heaven, and then inexplicably chose to fall down into hell. I no longer know why I behaved as I did, why I felt the way I did, why I could not see things straight.

I do know that I love you, and that I will never love like this again. I have hurt you intensely, I know that, too. I, at least, deserve my suffering. You don't. If I had not been so impetuous, if I had listened to you, and gone to a doctor earlier, I might not have lost the baby. I feel that what has happened has been a terrible punishment for my selfishness.

I don't know if you can find it in your heart to forgive me. If you can't, I will understand. You tried your best with me. I was too wild and too hurt to fit into what you expected of me. I have lost the great love of my life and it is all my fault.

I am being discharged from hospital tomorrow or later today. My parents want me to go to convalesce with them, but I cannot face them. I am going to stay with a friend here in town, Amanda John. Her address and phone number are at the top of this letter.

If you want me, I will be there. Please come to me, my love. I don't care if you rage at me, and call me every bad name you want to. I have earned them all. But come to me, and help me deal with this pain, because I don't think I can deal with it without you.

I love you always.

Your

Penny.

Reading her own stark words was like reading the final chapter of her own story, the tale of a woman whose pride was sometimes stronger than her love, and who had eventually found a love stronger than pride.

Her eyes blurred with tears.

'Do you remember writing those words?' he asked her.

'Yes,' she said. 'I remember now. I remember how I hated myself for my stupid pride. But Ryan, perhaps even then my pride was what stopped me from posting it—my inability to show you my true feelings and tell you how much I loved you.'

'We both needed time.'

'If I'd posted this letter, would you have come to me?' she whispered.

'Yes, of course,' he replied. 'You know I would have come.'

'Then things would have turned out very differently.'

'Yes, very differently. But perhaps not for the best.'

'What do you mean?' she asked, wiping the wetness from her cheeks.

'Perhaps we both needed that year apart to understand what we had lost,' Ryan said. 'I needed to learn that I had to listen to you. Give you space. Respect your ambitions, and help you try to achieve them, not insist you did things my way.'

'And I needed to learn that sometimes you do know what is best for me,' she said, smiling through her tears. 'That you are older and wiser, and that you understand me better than I understand myself.'

'Most of all,' he said, 'I think we both needed to understand how much we loved each other.'

Penny was in his arms and he was holding her tight. She kissed his mouth, whispering fiercely between kisses, 'I will never let you go again, my darling, never—never—never!'

'And I will never lose you again,' he said, his voice husky. 'I'll do whatever it takes to show you that I love you, adore you, worship you!'

'I love you so much, Ryan. I'm not going to mess it up again. Not this time!'

The things they had bought in Yorkshire arrived the following week. It was a hectically busy day, as Penny had not only to supervise the removals crew, and tell them where each piece was to go, but she was also in the middle of preparing for the Christmas dinner party at Northcote.

It was to be held in the formal dining room, a candlelit meal with all the trimmings—and Penny had decided that on this occasion she no longer wanted cooks or caterers to provide the food. She was going to make the meal herself in the glorious new kitchen—the first time it was being used for its intended purpose.

So when Ryan found her in the dining room, she was standing on a chair, issuing instructions to the butcher on one cellphone, talking to Ariadne on the other, directing the handyman on where to hang the two magnificent oil paintings, and keeping an eagle eye on the movers, who were carrying a priceless set of Hepplewhite furniture through to the drawing room.

'The transition to domestic goddess is complete,' he grinned. 'Have you got a moment for a humble mortal?'

'No requests for eternal life or the touch of gold,' she replied, 'I'm too busy. What is it, O beautiful mortal?'

'I wondered if the *Daily Echo* reaches Mount Olympus.' He passed her a copy of the newspaper. She glanced at the article he pointed to. It was headlined 'Professor Resigns University Post'.

She read through the brief item, then came down from her chair slowly.

'It says Tom has resigned his chair.'

Ryan nodded. 'He was fired. They've appointed a top American academic in his place. A woman. I don't think he'll be sorely missed.'

She recalled something Ryan had said to her recently, and looked at him. 'Did *you* have anything to do with this?'

'I don't think anybody should be able to destroy so much happiness and get away with it,' he replied. 'I think Tom got away with what he did because nobody wanted to talk about it. Well, I made sure that the right people did talk about it. That is all I did.'

'I've said it before—you are so machiavellian that it frightens me!'

'If I'd been in a different line of work, he might be sleeping with the fishes right now,' Ryan commented grimly. 'He should be grateful he's merely out of a job.'

She put her arms around his neck and kissed him on the

lips. 'Thank you for being my knight errant. But I feel a little bit sorry for him.'

'Don't,' he advised. 'He won't be able to prey on young women any more.' He glanced round the room. 'Those paintings are wonderful. You were right. This room is becoming spectacular.'

'Wait till Christmas Day,' she said. 'I'll show you spectacular!'

If she had really been a goddess, she could not have arranged the weather better.

There was a fresh snowfall just in time for Christmas Day. It covered the slush, leaving the world pure, holy and white.

By the evening, when their guests started to arrive, it had stopped snowing and cleared, and the sky was a glowing mass of stars shining down on a winter wonderland.

The great house had changed over the past days. It was not just that the treasures Penny and Ryan had put into it had made it look beautiful; it was something more subtle. The house, as Ryan had predicted, had become a home. Their home. A place for their dreams to be born, grow and mature.

The table glowed with flowers and candles. Penny had made a central display set out in one of the things they had bought at Havelock Hall, a huge silver tray. Because of its size and strange shape, the bidding had been low, despite the obvious value of the piece.

She had arranged a display of fruit, berries, flowers and green leaves around the base of a massive cluster of Christmas lilies. Rising from the centre were the tall, elegant necks of bird-of-paradise flowers.

Wreaths of holly and ivy were hung on the candelabra. She had also arranged posies of scented things—lavender, wild thyme and rosemary—at each place setting. There were crackers from Fortnum & Mason, party favours from Mappin & Webb and presents for everyone under the tree. The room looked and smelled delicious.

Penny checked swiftly to make sure everything was under control—full glasses, enough wine and champagne, a smile on every face.

It was a crowded table—there were twenty-four guests, some famous, some not, all people whom she and Ryan loved. Sitting beside her was Lucinda Strong. In the soft light, signs of age had been erased, and her face looked timeless and lovely.

'Do you still think that love consumes people?' she asked Penny in a low voice.

Penny shook her head. 'No, Lucinda. I've learned that true love replenishes and nourishes the soul. It can only make a person grow.'

Lucinda smiled. 'And have you learned who you are, yet?'

Penny hesitated before answering. 'No. But I've learned something more important. I've learned that I *don't* know who I am. I've stopped trying to pretend that I do, and making big decisions based on a silly idea of who I *want* to be. I'm learning to become myself.'

'Ah, then you've found wisdom since I saw you last,' Lucinda said. She laid her warm hand over Penny's. 'You and Ryan are so happy together. It's the two of you who are providing this wonderful light tonight. I'm so glad for you both.'

'I can't live without him,' she said simply.

'I don't think he can live without you,' Lucinda replied, glancing at Ryan across the table. 'Sometimes it's the things that cost us the most to achieve which are most important, in the end.'

Penny kissed Lucinda's soft cheek and slipped away from the table to check on the kitchen. The turkey had been taken out of the oven and was resting for the obligatory twenty minutes before being presented and carved. It looked perfect.

Tara, who was one of the guests but who had elected to help, was garnishing the serving dish with vegetables.

'I think we can take it in any time now,' Penny said.

'It looks wonderful,' Tara said. 'I've never seen such a spectacular Christmas turkey!'

'Hope it tastes as good as it looks,' Penny said, decorating the golden skin of the bird with holly.

Strong arms slipped around her waist and held her close.

'Everything you make tastes as good as it looks,' Ryan murmured in her ear.

She closed her eyes and leaned back against his broad chest. 'You're supposed to be back at the party, playing the genial host, entertaining our guests,' she said.

'Don't worry, they're having the time of their lives,' Ryan said. 'I just wanted to thank you for this wonderful night. You've worked so hard. Everything is so beautiful.'

'I'm happy that you're happy.' She turned to face him, and kissed him lingeringly on the lips. 'You've worked hard, too, my love.'

'Maybe that's the key,' he said. 'Both of us working hard. Making beautiful things happen, all our lives.'

'Are you going to tell them tonight?' she asked him.

'If you think so.'

'It's a good moment.'

'All right. I'll tell them now.'

They smiled into one another's eyes. No more words were necessary; they were talking to one another with their hearts and minds.

'What shall we do about the turkey?' Tara asked awkwardly, embarrassed by the silence.

'We'd better take it in,' Penny said, disengaging reluctantly from Ryan.

They carried the turkey in to applause from their guests.

Ryan made a great show of sharpening the carving knife, to laughter from their friends.

But before he began carving, he held up his hand.

'Penny and I want to thank you all for being here tonight,' he said. 'We want to wish you all a merry Christmas, too.'

There were happy words of response. When they had died down, Ryan held out his hand to Penny. She rose from her chair and took his hand.

'There's something else Penny and I want to say tonight. It's an announcement.' He smiled. 'You'd better tell them, Penny. They might not believe that I've been so lucky.'

'I'm the lucky one,' Penny said in a soft but clear voice. 'The most wonderful man in the world has asked me to be his wife. Ryan and I are going to be married in the New Year.'

There was a moment of silence. Then every single guest rose from his or her chair, applauding, and came to embrace them in turn.

'This is the loveliest Christmas present you could have given me,' Lucinda said, and there were tears in her eyes. 'God bless you both.'

They were married at Northcote in the spring. Big as the house was, it seemed too small to contain the number of guests who arrived to see them joined.

Yet the ceremony was simple. Were it not for the depth of love on both sides, which everyone assembled there could see at a glance, it might have seemed a plain wedding.

As it was, most of the guests said it was the most beautiful wedding they had ever attended.

Ryan and Penny were married under a bower of almond blossom. They exchanged rings and vows and the minister proclaimed them man and wife.

The snows of winter were long gone, and the green, green meadows of Northcote were bright with wild flowers under a blue sky. The guests, many of whom had come from other countries for the occasion, danced and feasted, or wandered around the great house, admiring the timeless beauty with which it had been furnished, renewing old friendships and fostering new ones.

Children played everywhere; party frocks were stained with fresh grass and party suits were torn clambering on the sensational jungle gym that Ryan and Penny had built on the lawn.

It was a day of joy and celebration.

The bride and groom danced together, never taking their eyes off one another, until their guests loudly demanded some attention, and they had to separate and mingle with the crowd, and bestow smiles on others.

But in the late afternoon Ryan took Penny's hand, and they slipped away from the festivities and ran upstairs to their bedroom, Penny holding her white organza gown up with her free hand.

He led her to the window, as he had once done months earlier, and they looked out.

This time, instead of moonlight and snow, the landscape was decorated with sunshine and flowers. A warm sun was shining down on their wedding guests, who thronged the gardens or danced to the strains of sweet old tunes.

The great trees, so old and mighty, wore headdresses of green leaves. But everything had the same unearthly beauty as it had that night, long ago, when she had tried to leave him behind, and had failed.

'Do you remember that you once told me I would tire of this place?' he asked her, taking her in his arms.

She smiled. 'Yes. I said you would want to be able to pop into Harrods for caviare and crackers.'

'I said then that I was too soon for you to understand. But I know you understand now.'

'Yes,' she said. 'I understand everything, my love. I know you bought this house for me. For our children to grow in. So we could make a life together in it.'

'I love you so much, Penny,' he said, looking into her eyes. 'It took us a long time and a lot of heartbreak to get here. But now that we are here, I know that it's been worth everything— and that I would do it again tomorrow, in a heartbeat.'

'Me, too,' she whispered, her mouth close to his.

Then they were lost in their kiss. The music of the orchestra drifted up to them from the flowery gardens below, and in that joyous melody there was no shadow that it would ever end again.

HARLEQUIN *Presents*

EXTRA

FORCED TO MARRY
Wives for the taking!

Once these men put a diamond ring on their bride's
finger, there's no going back....

Wedlocked and willful, these wives will get a
wedding night they'll never forget!

**Read all the fantastic stories, out this month
in Harlequin Presents EXTRA:**

The Santangeli Marriage #61
by SARA CRAVEN

Salzano's Captive Bride #62
by DAPHNE CLAIR

**The Ruthless Italian's
Inexperienced Wife #63**
by CHRISTINA HOLLIS

Bought for Marriage #64
by MARGARET MAYO

HARLEQUIN *Presents*

International Billionaires

Life is a game of power and pleasure.
And these men play to win!

THE SHEIKH'S LOVE-CHILD
by *Kate Hewitt*

When Lucy arrives in the desert kingdom of Biryal,
Sheikh Khaled's eyes are blacker and harder than
before. But Lucy and the sheikh are inextricably
bound forever—for he is the father of her son....

Book #2838
Available July 2009

Two more titles to collect in this exciting miniseries:
BLACKMAILED INTO THE GREEK
TYCOON'S BED by *Carol Marinelli*
August

THE VIRGIN SECRETARY'S
IMPOSSIBLE BOSS by *Carole Mortimer*
September

HARLEQUIN Presents

![Undressed]

Undressed
BY THE BOSS

From sensible suits…into satin sheets!

Even if at times work is rather boring,
there is one person making the office
a whole lot more interesting: the boss!

SHEIKH BOSS, HOT DESERT NIGHTS
by *Susan Stephens*

Casey feels out of her depth around her new boss!
Sheikh Rafik al Rafar likes a challenge, and seduces
Casey in the sultry heat—in time to learn that Casey
can teach him some simpler pleasures in life….

Book #2842
Available July 2009

**Look out for more of these supersexy titles
in this series!**
www.eHarlequin.com

HP12842

BROUGHT TO YOU BY FANS OF HARLEQUIN PRESENTS.

We are its editors and authors and biggest fans—and we'd love to hear from YOU!

Subscribe today to our online blog at
www.iheartpresents.com

REQUEST YOUR FREE BOOKS!

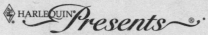

2 FREE NOVELS
PLUS 2
FREE GIFTS!

YES! Please send me 2 FREE Harlequin Presents® novels and my 2 FREE gifts (gifts are worth about $10). After receiving them, if I don't wish to receive any more books, I can return the shipping statement marked "cancel". If I don't cancel, I will receive 6 brand-new novels every month and be billed just $4.05 per book in the U.S. or $4.74 per book in Canada. That's a savings of close to 15% off the cover price! It's quite a bargain! Shipping and handling is just 50¢ per book*. I understand that accepting the 2 free books and gifts places me under no obligation to buy anything. I can always return a shipment and cancel at any time. Even if I never buy another book, the two free books and gifts are mine to keep forever.

106 HDN EYRQ   306 HDN EYR2

Name	(PLEASE PRINT)	
Address		Apt. #
City	State/Prov.	Zip/Postal Code

Signature (if under 18, a parent or guardian must sign)

Mail to the **Harlequin Reader Service**:
IN U.S.A.: P.O. Box 1867, Buffalo, NY 14240-1867
IN CANADA: P.O. Box 609, Fort Erie, Ontario L2A 5X3

Not valid to current subscribers of Harlequin Presents books.

Are you a current subscriber of Harlequin Presents books and want to receive the larger-print edition? Call 1-800-873-8635 today!

* Terms and prices subject to change without notice. Prices do not include applicable taxes. Sales tax applicable in N.Y. Canadian residents will be charged applicable provincial taxes and GST. Offer not valid in Quebec. This offer is limited to one order per household. All orders subject to approval. Credit or debit balances in a customer's account(s) may be offset by any other outstanding balance owed by or to the customer. Please allow 4 to 6 weeks for delivery. Offer available while quantities last.

Your Privacy: Harlequin Books is committed to protecting your privacy. Our Privacy Policy is available online at www.eHarlequin.com or upon request from the Reader Service. From time to time we make our lists of customers available to reputable third parties who may have a product or service of interest to you. If you would prefer we not share your name and address, please check here.

HP09R

You're invited to join our Tell Harlequin Reader Panel!

By joining our new reader panel you will:

- Receive Harlequin® books—they are FREE and yours to keep with no obligation to purchase anything!
- Participate in fun online surveys
- Exchange opinions and ideas with women just like you
- Have a say in our new book ideas and help us publish the best in women's fiction

In addition, you will have a chance to win great prizes and receive special gifts! See Web site for details. Some conditions apply. Space is limited.

To join, visit us at

www.TellHarlequin.com.